CAPSULE STORIES

Masthead

Natasha Lioe, Founder and Publisher
Carolina VonKampen, Publisher and Editor in Chief
April Bayer, Reader
Stephanie Coley, Reader
Rhea Dhanbhoora, Reader
Hannah Fortna, Reader
Kendra Nuttall, Reader
Rachel Skelton, Reader
Deanne Sleet, Reader
Claire Taylor, Reader

Cover art by Darius Serebrova
Book design by Carolina VonKampen

Paperback ISBN: 978-1-953958-10-5
Ebook ISBN: 978-1-953958-11-2

CAPSULE STORIES

Winter 2021 Edition

Sugar and Spice

Contents

Letter from the Editors

It's been a long year, and we all need an extra dose of cheer this winter. As 2021 closes, we want to reflect on happy memories of good food and the people we share it with. Inside this edition, you'll find stories and poems that feel cozy and warm and explore the ways food can bring us together during the winter holidays. Whether you sneak out of a joyous but loud family gathering to find comfort in these pages or crack open this book late at night with a plate of cookies and a cup of hot chocolate, we hope you enjoy reading about family traditions, recipes passed down through generations, and quiet moments of hope in these pages. Happy reading!

Prologue

Sugar and Spice

The room is warm when you wake up. Your body squeaks uncomfortably on an old leather sofa. Your little cousin is sitting on the rug of the living room, playing with his iPad. In a daze, you stumble toward the kitchen, toward the hearty laughter echoing through the hallways, the aunties arguing over oven space. Something smells like butter and garlic. You have been tasked with peeling potatoes.

Your family members bustle around the kitchen, stirring, tasting, adding more salt. A single potato slips out of your hands and bounces on the tile. You remember that you often feel alone at big gatherings. The inescapable urge to retreat to an empty bedroom. But what comforts you is imagining what is happening in all the other houses. You imagine a young woman, overdressed, sipping wine at the dining table by herself as chaos ensues around her. You imagine seventeen-year-olds being sent off to the grocery store for the third time in search of gravy packets and vanilla ice cream. You imagine some people must be alone, eating Chinese takeout, comforted by the quiet streets outside and the low hum of the radiator fixed to their apartment wall. The food is a string that ties us together, enriching small moments with a depth of flavor that will always remind you of home.

Ritual

Tamiko Dooley

Remind me of today
When the last flames flicker in the coals
And the room begins to dim and cool

Play the jingles we've heard too many times
Feed me mince pies that burn my lips
Carrots oversweetened with honey

Place a paper crown on my head
Tell me a joke I already know
Lay a cloth napkin on my knees

This December day will cheer me
As twinkling lights in windows
Warm a passerby trudging through the snow outside.

The Chesapeake's Cornucopia

Annie Marhefka

In Baltimore, there are five seasons: winter, spring, summer, autumn, and tailgating season, that gap between crunchy russet leaves and ice-tipped blades of parched grass.

It is tailgating season in Baltimore and for our family, that means more than Thanksgiving or Christmas or weddings or college graduations. It means extensive lists and shopping trips and ticket distribution, and the annual tune-up of our tailgate van, which only ever travels from my father's house to the football stadium, and back, on Sundays. On Saturdays, he takes her for a test drive around the neighborhood—a superstitious errand, more about calming his pregame nerves than checking her rusty brakes. She is painted a base coat of black underneath a gloss speckled with violet metallic flakes that cast a glittery shadow when the sun catches them just right. Her license plate reads simply: GAMEDAY. Her inner floor is carpeted with an emerald-green Astroturf, and the long, crackling leather seats are positioned around the sides, where the tailgaters will huddle and sit atop one another's laps, allowing more space for the critical gear.

The equipment is stacked in the center—the grill, the plastic bins of organized supplies, the propane tank, the steamer pot large enough to hold a twelve-pound turkey. The propane tank is technically not permitted as a passenger in the van as we travel through the tunnel that parts the waters of Baltimore's Inner Harbor. The tunnel's drab tiles are dimly lit with the yellowed glow of scattered bulbs, but we lean forward to block the propane tank's view from the tollbooth operator before slipping inside the tunnel's berth.

We emerge from the tunnel and arrive at precisely nine o'clock, the moment the parking lot attendants check their wristwatches and shuffle forward to slide the heavy wooden gate from the lot's entrance. Our arrival is meticulously timed, as always, and we flash our parking pass as we pull forward. My father eases the van into her regular spot between the chalky white lines. My Uncle Jack hops out of the front passenger seat and opens the double doors along the side of the van.

We all pile out, each taking Jack's hand as we navigate around the piles of tailgate gear, jumping out the side like obedient soldiers in a line. We carry the items out of the van with assembly-line precision: the grill is a two-person job, followed by the folding tables, the chairs we never sit in, and the foil-covered aluminum tins of food. We set into motion—Jack and my cousin unfolding the tables and snapping the locking mechanisms into place. My mother and I determine the order of the food offerings on the tables—appetizers first on the left, followed by main dishes and sides, then dessert. My father warms up the grill and positions the steamer pot and propane tank a safe distance from the van. We each have our setup duties.

Except Adam. Adam always steps aside, tugging a small glass bottle of whiskey out of his cargo pants pocket. We know he has nerves like my father, and an affinity for the taste of Old Grand-Dad on Sunday mornings.

The setup is simpler today, mostly appetizers resting on chafing dishes above warming flames. The table that holds the appetizers is adorned with a homemade tablecloth stitched by my mother's arthritic hands—a deep purple cotton spotted with the Baltimore Ravens' black-winged emblem.

The other table, the longest one, we cover with brown paper, recognizable to anyone from Baltimore as crab-picking paper. We have a theme for each game's menu—Philly cheesesteaks and soft pretzels when we play the Eagles, an Oktoberfest tailgate with bratwursts and German potato salad, and a full Thanksgiving spread in November, complete with turkeys and stuffings and pies.

Today we are having our once-a-year seafood steamer feast. We always reserve the seafood tailgate for the coldest gameday of the year. This is that day. The temperature will dip low, and the clouds will shield the sun from providing any warmth. We have all checked the forecast daily leading up to Sunday, hoping for a shift, a reprieve that isn't offered. It's going to be a brutal day to spend outside. We have all dressed in layers—long johns and leggings under jeans or snow pants; thick socks and single-use heating packets stuffed into our boots; hats and scarves, mittens and earmuffs.

The four hours pass by slowly, filled with the same patterns, Sunday after Sunday. My mother always seeks out the mobile lottery booth, buys too many twenty-dollar-a-pop scratch-off tickets, squeals with a winner's joy when one of them yields a ten-dollar prize. My father is always the grill-master, donning a black apron that reads Real Men Fry Turkeys, a set of metal tongs ever-present in his right hand. We each have a wine glass, custom etched with our names, that we pull from a large bin in the back of the van and sip from for those four hours, returning the lip-stained rims and stems to the bin for my mother to wash later. Every week, a homeless man approaches timidly, and each time my father slips him a twenty and a plate heaped with food. I wonder if he looks forward to the seafood tailgate each season like we do.

The seafood steams in the pot as we sip our wine and snack on grilled tuna steaks with my father's special wasabi sauce mixture. Dad has carefully layered the shells—the clams, mussels, and crab legs—between rows of corn on the cob and sliced onions. And throughout the pot, the Old Bay Seasoning blend is sprinkled evenly. Its layers are as carefully thought out as my Italian great-grandmother's lasagna, and its seasoning is the secret sauce no one can seem to replicate. We talk and sip and rub our gloved hands together for warmth as we watch the needle on the pot lid tick upward. My father never walks more than a few feet away from the pot, keeping an eye on it as he tends to the grill and his family. And then finally, he declares it is ready.

He trades his wool gloves for rubber ones designed to protect his machinist hands from the heat of the metal handles on the pot. He lifts the large pot from its base, and we all take a few steps back as he hefts it over the table, tilts it downward, and lets the contents spill over the brown-papered table: the Chesapeake Bay's cornucopia.

The heat of the mollusks' shells meets the bitter cold winter air and swirls tiny tornadoes of steam upward, covering the air above the table like a fog. My father, the only one of us on the far side of the table, is blurred from our view by the Old Bay-scented vapors but still we know he is grinning as the aroma travels across the parking lot, lifting noses of nearby tailgaters and forcing them to turn their rosy cheeks in our direction.

I stand ready with a fistful of forks at the head of the table, and one by one, the tailgaters take their utensils from me and circle up around the table. One fork is all we need—we remove our gloves and mittens and warm our hands instead with the shells of the clams and mussels and crab legs. At a nice seafood restaurant in Baltimore, we might use a delicate crab knife or a wooden mallet, but here we tear into our pile of shelled sea edibles with our bare fingers. We let our hands do the breaking and pulling, and then scoop out our treasure with the forks. There are bowls of butter that have been warmed on the grill, and we dip our morsels in and out of the creamy butter melt before settling them onto our lips.

The reddish-brown seasoning will creep under our fingernails and remain there throughout the game, wafting that familiar smell throughout the stadium's stands as we clap and roar with excitement. The satisfying crack of the exoskeleton releases a stream of salt-tinged heat into our faces, and the soft meat melts into our tongues.

It's tailgating season in Baltimore, and yes, there is a game today, but this—this is what we came for.

Over the years, we will all change; the bodies we are residing in will change. My father's beard will turn from black to gray to white, but the Old Bay will still cling to its wiry hairs just the same. There will be years when the bay is dried up of crabs, and we import king crab claws to take their place, and then other years when the bay's harvest is plentiful again, like the neighbor who can't give away all his garden-grown cucumbers in late summer.

I will quit eating meat, and our menu will start including more vegetarian and pescatarian options—mushroom caps stuffed with blends of cheese, jalapeño poppers, and oysters. I will have a baby, after a season of avoiding the seared tuna, still pink in the middle, and overindulging in the cakes and pies toward the end of the tailgate. I won't come to as many games after my daughter is born, even though I said I would pre-motherhood, choosing peekaboo and drool-covered bibs over a day away from the miniature version of me.

My mother will die, unexpectedly, and we will go on using her handmade tablecloth and plastic utensil caddies. Her etched wine glass will stay in the bin, and we will still buy scratch-off tickets from the mobile lottery stand for her, taking turns rubbing the filmy surface off with quarters, and celebrating her small wins.

My uncle's embrace will morph from a jolly squeeze to a longer, more comforting reassurance. My father will start reaching for my hand as we enter the stadium, and I will clutch his back in solidarity.

We will change, but this—this will remain constant. We will still gather here around this table and feast, letting the salty steam swathe us in an immersion of nostalgia and a kinship of all those years passed, all those times we warmed each other with clams, and whiskey, and knowing looks.

we will still gather here
around this table and feast

Home-Baked

Ellen Clayton

Christmas Eve and my parents' house is
cacophonous.
Twenty of us, squeezed in to precious bricks
and mortar, the foundations of our family.
I duck out to the garage,
cold air blasting my face as I open the door
to retrieve the champagne that's chilling,
away from the toasty kitchen.
I pause on the threshold before I reenter,
surveying the scene.
A room ablaze with warmth and cheer;
all those I hold dear
gathered in garish Christmas jumpers.
The table, cloaked with the red tablecloth
used just two days a year,
is heaving, brimming with buffet delights,
and the star attraction is yet to be served:
Mum's home-baked spicy sausage rolls—
the scent of them cooking
makes my mouth water in anticipation.

I close the door to the garage,
keeping the chill from entering our festive haven,
breathe in deeply:
feel myself thaw,
coming home.
I pour the drinks then
my brother and I hover by the oven,
waiting for Mum to declare her sausage rolls done
so we can pounce.

The Christmas music is barely audible over
simultaneous conversations
and my champagne glass is suddenly empty,
quaffed down too quickly
in the buzz and hubbub of my favorite day of the year.
My children cram crisps and hummus
into small fists, giddy on the promise
of Father Christmas and his impending arrival,
excitedly laughing with their older cousins.

Outside a bitter wind blows and darkness
shrouds the garden
but this kitchen is
enveloped in light.
Finally, it is time.
The sausage rolls are ready
and I have grabbed two,
contemplating for a moment
exactly how long I have to wait
to avoid burning my mouth.
I bite in, perfectly crisp pastry
flaking over my lips onto the plate
as warm, tender meat flecked with the
fiery kick of jalapeños
floods my mouth with a taste sensation.
I grin at Mum, gleefully shrieking
"The best ones yet!" as I am
sated
with love and hot sausage rolls.

breathe in deeply:
feel myself thaw,
coming home

Just a Quick Nap

Sean Wang

The first frost dusts the leaves
with a tinkle. Bells of pine
dawdle around the table like gnomes.
The oven purrs, snuggling a turkey crackling like a log.
I pour myself a glass of eggnog and wince at the pinch of brandy.
I must have opened the wrong bottle—
my cheeks have an impish glow, overstuffed
with sweet potatoes and cranberries
like a squirrel, ready for the winter ahead.
Outside, the snow forms spirals like a chandelier,
each flake strung up, refracting the sun's glint
like a champagne flute, stacked and bubbling.
Sleep curls around me like a sweater
woolly and fleeced, I stumble to the sofa,
which my spaniel has made into a nest.
The cushions nibble on me like a peppermint cookie.
The kitchen is rumbling
as cutlery, dishes and tablecloths settle onto the table.
As the snow shifts into mounds, snowmen spring up like gifts.
I feel myself melting like gingerbread in a glass of warm milk,
the house crumbles away.
My skin pricks with the soft kiss of the fireplace,
I listen to the wind whirr like the sea
washing in tides of foam-white snow.
In an hour the house will be bursting with people,
and we'll sit around tables heaped with food
drifting in a womb of snow
ready to be birthed into the new year.
The laughter pumps through the dark night like a heartbeat.

Recipe

Ciera Horton McElroy

Make the soup first. Drop silky eggs into stock and whisk. Spin a whirlpool. It's all in the wrist. Add salt by the pinch, by the fistful. Layer the ginger in tiny paper sheets. Mix until the color of creamed corn. Savor the steam, the music, groceries piled on the counter, wine pouring into glasses. The wine is cheap, but any wine will do.

This is a dinner party: Chinese, Jewish, American.

You will ache for a larger home for hosting. Instead, what you have is a one-bedroom apartment. An IKEA table that you did not buy from IKEA but Facebook Marketplace for half price. There is a nail-shaped gouge on the veneer. Perfect for a strategically placed vase. You will apologize for the smallness, the elbow-to-elbow kitchen. Don't. This is where you are in life: graduate school, newlywed, stipends and scholarships. You do not have a lot. But you have this: friends around your thrifted table, food on your stove.

So accept it. Enjoy. There are four people in a kitchen made for one. Love it, even, how your home feels full and loud and thick with garlic. Step aside. Let your guest use the sink. Let him wash the potato eyes. Help him grate the russets into tiny oat flakes. You will learn a new thing today, how to coat and fry potatoes in flour, and you will never think of Easter without latkes again.

When you realize that latkes call for applesauce, resolve to make some. Google how. Watch a video, then peel an apple. Dice and microwave and pulse in the blender. Dash with cinnamon, place in a bowl.

Let the soup simmer and the sun set. Do not eat until the light is right, until it's dark and golden like stove-warmed honey.

Serve the challah first. Serve it with sesame seeds. Serve it with butter. Spoon falafel from sunflower oil on the stove, piping hot, still bubbling. Take in the beauty before you eat: apricots and dates, pita chips with paprika. You spent your paycheck on food, but this is good. Food is something to share.

This is a dinner for the allergic. It is nut free, fish free. This is a dinner for disagreement: talk about Jesus and Jerusalem and ethics. About medicine and family and Hong Kong. Talk about silly things: gossip and friends and who's dating who. The best pho in town, sex scandals, the president. Talk about nothing. Open another bottle, take second helpings. Play a board game or don't. Sit and be still, light another candle. Because this? This is not something you will always have, the ability to gather—to double-dip without thinking, to forget whose wine glass is whose and not really care. Forget about the crumbs on the floor and the gouge on the table. Forget, please, about assignments and money and having perfect plates. No one cares as much as you do. Everyone just wants to eat.

everyone just
wants to eat

In Our Kitchen on Christmas Eve

Jen Feroze

You turn from the counter holding a cheeseboard like a newborn at the font. We sit hushed and ready to be transported, as is tradition. You take us with you to the mushroomed damp of the cheese caves; to those first shuddering milkings when frothing buckets wobble with starlight. As you do each year, you show us the Langres, fingers fluttering as you mimic washing it in eau-de-vie. You point to the knots and whirls of blue in the Roquefort, tell us its pale, salty folktale. There's the Comté, cared for in cool storerooms for nearly two years, hiding salt crystals like seams of quartz. There's the Brie de Meaux, sighing with the weight of its creaminess, its forest floor tang. There's your mother and a guillotine flash of impatience. There's her slow, enraptured smile. And, darling, how you flinch as if it were your own skin.

I am full. And yet I eat
pieces of farmhouse gold
from the palm of your hand.

Solace

Charlotte Gutzmer

Somewhere wrapped in wildwood, a farmhouse crouches
below ceramic stars, glazed moon, trees shrouded in crystalline
snow. Foggy winter slumbers in the valley, stillness fragmented
only by the light in our windows.

Here, we've kindled the fire to dance around us,
spectacular waltzes of orange and pink, flames licking
our scraped knees. I feed my lover cherries, pomegranates,
flavors bursting and dripping in sweetness.

Her hands at the nape of my neck, small of my back, pressing
heat through my skin. It's saved my life to know these hands,
to know the impressions of ghosts and fingerprints they leave
behind.

It's the lazy circles she draws down my spine, flurries
of movement like falling snow. It's the survival instinct,
the taste of buttercream and cocoa lingering
on our tongues, kisses printed up my jaw—

Somewhere, the trees shrug off their snow, bending to glimpse
the halation of life unfurling from our windows.

in the house under the snow

Aral L.

1:43 a.m. and the night
forgot itself.
no longer a strange creature
making the hairs
on our arms prickle with its exhales.
no longer sharp
and heavy.
the night forgot itself and
wrapped its infinite arms around
our blanketed bodies.
mugs warmed hands and
skin warmed skin and
candles warmed darkness and—
i told you i'd make you a cup of tea.
you asked if there'd be honey.
i said yes,
there would be honey.

Let It Be

Jaime Dill

If love has a flavor
let it be the cinnamon
on the rim of your chai tea,
hovering between the table
and your lips as they interrupt
your thirst with arguments
of literary hunger.

We spill these feelings
over lacquered tabletops,
surrounded by frosted panes
and whisps of Bing Crosby vinyl,
caught up in a seasonal rush
of gifting precious things,
like the details of our smiles
and childhood memories.

We can meet a million times,
but it's never quite like this—
breathing in the magic of
fleece weather and fireplace crackles.
In days of long Decembers,
our bodies attach to warmth,
making your laugh sound like
tinkles of sanctuary and
your candlelit face look like home.

If love is a holiday,
let it be the combination
of our highs through the year,

gathered into words of thanks
as the months wrap us up
in memories of where we've been
amid piles of new dreams,
like the lucky snow days that
fall right when we need a
Hallmark moment to land
on our faces and remind us
there are things worth believing in.

gifting precious things,
like the details of our smiles
and childhood memories

Growing Pains

Amanda Hurley

Her daughter is ill again, the usual, recurring stomachache that seems to have no cause. In vain, she's had her tested for allergies, watched as the doctor drew twelve faint scratches into her daughter's skin and then applied traces of wheat, dairy, animal hair. She's seen her daughter poked and prodded, stethoscopes held against that pale back now covered by a scatter of freckles, the cold wand of the ultrasound pressed icily against her daughter's beautiful rounded stomach. That same stomach that she once tickled as she changed a dirty diaper, now hidden behind a pair of loose ripped jeans, an eagle's head buckle to hold them in place. The child that's now a teenager, the traces of the baby she once was visible only to her mother's worried eye.

Her daughter is lying on the bed, a hot water bottle clamped to her waist, bent into a fetal position, missing only a thumb inside her mouth. She stands at the door, hovers, unable to soothe her daughter's churning insides, a pain so sharp, it's sent her home from school early after a visit to the nurse. She wishes she knew more about her daughter's daily life, if there are other children that are unkind to her, if she finds the work she's assigned by the teachers too taxing. If she's anxious about having to speak in front of the class, twenty-four pairs of eyes watching her every move as she stands before the blackboard, her carefully compiled assignment clasped in a clammy hand. When she asks her daughter these questions, she meets a stony wall of single syllables and there's a tenseness in her daughter's eyes, warning her about pushing too close. She can handle this, her daughter's eyes say, she's okay, let her be.

But her daughter's not okay, this much she's allowed to see. The regular cramps unrelated to her cycle. The sick days piling up on the school's report card. Is it a spiritual malaise that's breaking into the physical? Something psychological that's disturbing her body's equilibrium? Or is it that there's something drastically, physically wrong, an illness that is cutting into her daughter's guts? She's yet to find a doctor who can tell her.

She goes into the kitchen, uncovers the chicken from the tea towel that has been protecting it while it warms to room temperature. Taking a wad of kitchen paper, she pats the bird dry, reaching inside the socket between its entwined legs to remove the giblets packed in plastic. Then with practiced fingers, she rips the meat into shreds, dropping each piece into the steaming broth she'd started preparing earlier after the phone call from the school to let her know her daughter was on her way home. There are slices of red onion in there, cubes of carrot and spherical peas that have turned bright green from the heat of the soup. In a while, she'll shake in a decent serving of salt and dried herbs, and add freshly rinsed rice to the brew, waiting until the mineral-rich broth has entered each grain. She'll let it cool in the bowl slightly, the fat from the meat congealing on the soup's surface, a pale rainbow of oil, before bringing it in to her daughter. It's her mother-in-law's recipe and the only thing she can get her daughter to eat when her stomach is giving her hell.

She knocks gently as she enters her daughter's room, curtains pulled against the graying winter's day. She's slipped off into a dreamless sleep and there's nothing to be done except to place the steaming bowl of soup onto the desk and to tiptoe to her daughter's bed, to draw the blanket higher up over her shoulders, to pause briefly to check her daughter's breath. To see in her mind's eye her daughter's red rosy cheeks as the first teeth pushed their way through her tender gums, remembering the helplessness she felt then, unable to shelter her daughter from those very first growing pains.

She returns to the kitchen, a cooling cup of tea awaiting her as she slips into a chair at the table. She sits uneasily, keeping the soup warming on the stove, condensation gathering on the windowpane above. Waits until her daughter awakens and needs her.

Worcester, Christmas 1996

Ceinwen E Cariad Haydon

We knew you'd soon be gone,
choices had been made. Ashes
choked our grate, and we lacked
the will to sweep it clean, to lay
new fires to warm our hands.
Divorce would follow the holiday.

My son, back from wandering,
took my hand, led me outside.
We walked and talked until
tired, then headed for the pub.
Held by a squash of bodies,
our beers lapped over glasses
as we sipped. I heard a voice
and turned, saw my old friend.
I smiled, he drew us to free chairs,
we chatted and caught up. I heard
he needed help on Christmas Day,
when his shelter opened doors
to feed all who had nowhere to stay.

My lad and I signed up to celebrate
with men and women of the road.
What started as a time of emptiness
became an overflow of kindness.

At New Year when we parted, love,
I drew on this to wish you all the best—
and dry wood to build fresh, living fires.

Winter Market, Galway

Steve Denehan

We held our fingers to our lips
took a drag
exhaled
watched the smoke
from our invisible cigarettes
hang in the night air

I don't know why people smoke
when they can do this
my daughter said

we walked on
through the people and the lights
bought some homemade fudge
drank some warm mulled wine

came upon a fruit seller
a strange thing for a winter market
yet the colors were so vivid
the fruit so perfect
works of art almost

there was a pyramid
of Red Delicious apples
utterly out of season
a heart, between beats, was perched at the top
Christmas reflecting in its cartoon sheen
I picked it up by the stem
said to the seller
Summer in winter!

his expression did not change
One euro
I gave it and he took it and he looked away
we walked on
Some people aren't very happy, Dad
I squeezed her hand
took a bite of the apple
it was bitter

the fruit so perfect
works of art almost

French Toast Breakfast

Steve Denehan

There were years when I felt the tug of it
the questions, the cajoling
the odd social pressure of how
to see in the new year

only once, maybe twice
did I find myself counting down
smiling, hard as I could
with acquaintances
old and new
I did try to buy into it
tried to feel
what everybody else
seemed to feel

we made our phone calls early yesterday
settled down to an evening film
chosen by my daughter
about a spy
a real tough cookie
who befriends a little girl
it was pretty terrible
it was pretty fantastic

we filled up on goodies
leftover Christmas chocolates
never solving the mystery
of who kept leaving
the empty wrappers
in the tin

later on, as her eyes grew heavy
we did it, we counted down
cheering at the stroke of midnight
I don't feel any different
Neither do I

we woke late today
the world was clear and bright
there was French toast for breakfast
a new year
another new year

we woke late today
the world was clear
and bright

Red Bean, Chrysan-themum

Rachel Kim

Parting my lips slightly, I blew a soft white dragon through the frigid air of wintery Seoul, sharing the warmth of my cheeks for it to dissolve into fleeting flight. A single window in the office buildings above twinkled briefly, as if my dragon had joined ranks as a newborn star—The First Noel. I lowered my gaze from the steel heavens and buried my chin back into a pilling wool scarf. The end of the street was near. I clutched the hand warmer in my pocket, prowling forward to stuff myself with a Korean winter.

Hotteok. As I finally crossed through the busy intersection, colorful tents of crinkling tarp and trucks with their sides propped open like petite planes shimmered with light and steam on each side of the carless road. I quickly reached the line leader, holding out a cerulean dollar bill.

"One seed hotteok, please." Worked by deft hands, a glutinous rice dough ball was filled with sugar and toasted seeds, placed on a grill layered with scalding oil, and pressed down into a flat, round disc. A line forming behind me, multiple full moons rose onto the sizzling gray backdrop. I soon received my circular treasure, folded, in a small paper cup. Each piping hot mouthful dripped with caramelized sugar, rich honey brown. Hotteok, sweet pancake.

Gunbam. Nearby, feverish sparks flew from the sides of a vented barrel, spinning with a dull drum like peppering hail. Within, a mahogany batch of chestnuts whirled together in dry heat, popping like gilded hearts, their burnt sienna skin chipping away to reveal golden flesh. As the chestnuts tumbled into a paper pouch, a comforting aroma infused every breath. I eagerly delved in, almost searing the tips of my fingers. Gunbam, roasted chestnut.

Bungeoppang. A pair of high school girlfriends, both wearing black puffer jackets that reached down to their ankles, jokingly scoffed at each other in front of the bungeoppang truck. A serious contest on the superiority of red bean filling or cream filling was at the center of their debate, but intermittent laughter betrayed the solemn argument. As if to remain neutral, I stepped aside and asked for a bag of bungeoppang, half-half. Fluffy yet chewy buns, shaped to look like fish and filled with either sweet red bean paste or choux cream, dove into a thin paper bag. Cradling the warm pouch in my jacket kangaroo-style, I picked off the plump fish from fin to fin. Bungeoppang, fish-shaped bun.

Gukhwappang. Following the faint tinkling of metal on metal, I arrived at batter poured into shallow wells in a large griddle. Each pool of batter, containing a dollop of smooth red bean paste, was flipped over by a thin metal skewer when nearly cooked through. Resembling thick, golden pastry coins imprinted with a chrysanthemum on both heads and tails, a heavy bag of gukhwappang in winter was a sack of riches. Selecting from my own hefty share, I cautiously bit into a blistering bloom as its escaping steam spiraled through the cold. Gukhwappang, chrysanthemum bread.

Ggochi eomuk. Savory, salty broth washes over my saccharine tongue. I lift the wooden skewer that pierces through ivory waves of fish cake, nibbling on the soupy end. As the winter night comes to a close, I am filled with a languid glow. The twinkling star watches over me. Ggochi eomuk, skewered fish cake.

I am filled with a languid glow

candied haws and other sweet things about new year's

Luna Yin

i've forgotten how much i missed
the tart sweetness of candied hawthorn
fat red berries skewered on a thin wooden stick
shining with sugared glaze

mama looks the other way as i swipe one from the counter
too busy watching the dumplings bobbing in the boiling pot
plump and warm as the rosy cheeks
of the children playing outside,
their breath swirling in the frosty air like
the steam of the round white buns cooking in the kitchen

the crunch of small feet on icy snow now accompanied by
cries of amazement and surprise as
baba lights up the firecrackers outside,
brilliant light flashing in the evening air,
the sound of exploding sparks echoing across the cold sky

mama has to yell over our shouts of awe to call us back inside
she lays a steamed fish sprinkled with soy sauce and herbs
down on the table
and my little sister asks about when the fish was alive,
swimming in circles like the thin leaves floating in
nainai's green tea

nainai sips from her porcelain cup and continues her story,
another folk legend, colored with magic
as vivid and exciting as the red envelopes
mama and baba press into our exuberant little hands

the bright light and bright laughter of the house
flood through the windows into the dark winter night,
from above, the stars twinkle as if they are laughing with us,
the full moon smiling with a softly golden glow
perhaps it is also wishing us
a happy lunar new year

the bright light
and bright laughter
of the house
flood through the windows
into the dark winter night

Kentucky Blackberry Jam Cake

Kay Miller

Whenever I stop at a railroad crossing for a train to pass, I think of blackberry jam cake. My grandmother would make her version of the southern classic when we'd visit her cottage in a small, rural town built along the Ohio River. To the north was a steel mill, and to the east and west, the foothills of the Appalachian Mountains. Grandmother lived in southern Ohio, but she was born in Kentucky and so was the blackberry jam cake recipe. It's an old-fashioned dessert made during the holidays, although it'd be tasty any time of year. The cake batter includes heaps of butter, sugar, eggs, walnuts, and an assortment of spices; a small jar of homemade blackberry jam and a cup of buttermilk provide tangy notes to the sweet batter. Caramel icing crowns the cooled cake, enticing even the strictest calorie counter to have a generous slice.

Scents of cinnamon, allspice, and clove circulate around my grandmother's tiny kitchen and make their way into the far corners of her two-bedroom cottage. My siblings and I stand outside the arched doorway separating her cozy living room from the kitchen and peer inside to see three unassembled cake layers cooling on a wire rack. We are anxious for a taste, but that is several hours away.

To pass the time, we don our coats, hats, boots, and gloves and leave the warmth of the woodburning flagstone fireplace inside, heading into the blustery winds and swirling snowflakes outdoors. Snowballs sail back and forth, heads duck, cries of revenge ensue until a truce, suggested by my eldest sibling, to build our version of Frosty. The snowman's lumpy body is two-thirds complete when we hear the long, forlorn wail of a train whistle. We whoop and holler with glee and run to the edge of our grandmother's property. Black B&O railroad cars loaded with coal meander down the tracks with accompanying squeaks, shrill clanks, and the clickety-clack of the wheels on the imperfect rails. Our excitement mounts as the train nears the end. We jump up and down, waving our arms above our stocking-capped heads, making sure the conductor in the dark-red caboose sees us standing across the ravine. He spots us and gives a hearty wave through the square glass window of his compartment.

We return to our grandmother's kitchen excited and hungry. She helps us shed our outerwear and hangs each wet garment to a line stretched across her compact utility room. Boots line up like soldiers on the linoleum floor below. She kisses the tops of our damp heads and herds us into the kitchen, offering steaming hot cocoa. We sip the rich chocolaty drink while eyeing the three-tiered cake over the rims of our mugs. She grins as she pulls a long serrated knife out of the drawer and slices pieces of cake off the plate. Whipped caramel peaks top the berry-hued chunks, their insides speckled with chopped walnuts and tiny blackberry seeds. The generous slices disappear from our plates quicker than the B&O train does from the winter landscape, but the memories of my siblings and grandmother, seated at a kitchen table sprinkled with cake crumbs and stories, last a lifetime.

She kisses the tops
of our damp heads

offering steaming
hot cocoa

Hello My Darlin'

Lizzie Thornton

The light breaks in through the cracks of the curtains
resting on my pillow-creased skin.
I wake slowly, then all at once, remembering we are finally back.
I sense the stillness in the chilly air and then I smell it—
fragrant beans, heavily burned
caramelized roasted toffee
Hershey's on a woodburning fireplace.
My grandma smiles
Hello my darlin'
and hands me a cup.
The coffee smells like late-night card games
and early-morning cuddles.
The mug is hot as I press my palms around it
but I don't move until the heat becomes familiar and safe.
We drink two cups until the others wake
and gather around the tree for presents.

Textbooks, paper, and pens crowd the small, wooden table.
The light from the laptop glows, the soft trickle of the coffee
can be heard if you listen closely.
It's hot and bitter.
It screams *stay awake!*
A smooth finish of nutty butter lingers on my lips and
for a moment
I think of the swing on the porch with my grandma and
the coffee mug with the pink lips that I love.
Heat burns my fingers lightly as I remember and breathe
the sweet, sweet smell of safety, of unconditional love.
She believes in me like I believe the coffee will keep me up.
I smile, exhale, and get back to work.

French Press

A. M. Arndt

This place makes me think of Christmas,
with its faux European feel.
The artificial, shaped topiaries stacked like green ornaments
reflect Riviera *and* holiday flavor.
Accents of burgundy and gold surround a fire,
the heart of the place,
this warm nest out of the elements.
Sumptuous aromas envelop patrons
that push into the heat to retreat from the outer cold.
It's December, and festive spice is in the air.
I have an idea that Santa's workshop is somewhere
back there behind the coffee counter.
The sounds from that direction
only confirm my suspicions.
I wonder if they're hiring—
if the pretense they play at pays extra.
A far cry from elves,
yet employee headsets and impossibly small aprons
lend to the hazy illusion of a tiny workforce
hidden in the steam of the streamlined espresso machine.
A grownup's Polar Express sits in the station, chuffing;
it carries us—
in the same dream-drunken stupor of childhood—
to wakefulness, to a morning that feels like Christmas
in a warm café in December.

Potato Season

Wendy BooydeGraaff

In today's quiet hum of furnace and plates
clinking, I try to write one perfect
sentence that hums its own beauty of the
ordinary and echoes with universal
resonance. It doesn't have to be long.
My daughter sits beside me. Five words
that are precise and whole. My daughter
sits beside me silently while I write
and she waits. Twelve words. You don't
know the beauty of this, her urgent trembling
to speak, the way she is holding back the
waterfall of words she might forget so I can write
these sentences that will never express
the perfection of this moment.

Devotions

Sara Davis

There is only a short window of time to buy quinces. In other, more ordinary years, those were the transitional days at the end of October: crisp blue skies, broad beams of sunlight, crates of yellow-green globes at the outdoor market.

What are you going to do with those, a farmer asked me the first time I filled my arms with them. Do you know how to cook them, is what he meant. Quince jam, I told him. Quinces preserved in the autumn meant jewellike quince tarts for winter holiday parties. Spiced quince almond cake for my partner's birthday, lightly drenched in vanilla bean syrup. Slices of rosy quince crumble with our tea on snowy days. A love language, is what I meant.

This year, the quinces come in a wax-coated box filled with other local fruits and vegetables, delivered to my door with a brisk knock. The driver is usually back in his truck when I open the door; we wave, eyes crinkling above our masks. He's usually the only other person I see on Wednesdays.

I leave the quinces on my kitchen counter. Around them, life quietly ticks on.

By the third day, the kitchen smells of honey and flowers. The quinces are still hard but have deepened to a golden yellow. I cut them into quarters to make it easier to remove the peel and spongy pips, then cut the quarters into thin slices. The controlled movement of the knife releases a fine spray of floral fragrance: a kitchen prayer. On the stove, a transformation: the pearly white flesh cooks low and slow and sweet; it softens and flushes pink.

Every spoonful like a sunset, coral and amber and rose. This year I eat it alone.

Holy Night

Philip Styrt

When all outside is endless, empty white
Except the footprints of the frantic dog
Who scampers in ecstatic epilogue
To her own business; when the dark of night
Falls early, and reveals only the light
Of neighbor windows lit by their Yule log;
When even normal breathing will befog
The glass; when our fond Fahrenheit
Dips into numbers Celsius prefers;
That's when I find myself the most inclined
To cuddle up—in winter no one stirs—
With blankets on and pillows stacked behind
And watch the wind sweep through the white-tipped firs
With tea-warmed fingers and a quiet mind.

cinnamon

Alexandra Weiss

setting sun yolk running over
blue shadow canvas
the snow-covered park
did i walk past you rehearsing summer
shakespeare? i wonder
blue christmas lights left on
i come home to them and your cologne
hangs in the air
and you didn't leave when i told you
why the tattoos are where they are
you kissed my wrist
and everything's still blue but
you make me laugh
and everything's still blue but
you make hot chocolate with cinnamon
and you come back every night

Baking Do

Kalisse L. Van Dellen

2 cups cake flour (not self-rising)

I don't have cake flour. I have a tub of white flour, a mason jar of buckwheat, and a crumpled bag of whole wheat flour that I think is a different protein percentage than the brand I grew up with in Canada. The sensible thing to do would be to Google a different recipe or run to the Sprouts market 0.9 miles up the road. I can't do either.

I need to bake from this cookbook today. *The Epicurious Cookbook*. I got it from my sister, Kate, last Christmas. She watched me open it from a locked-down province three thousand miles away. She might be the only person who remembers that I used to bake weekly. I haven't baked much recently, but Kate knows I can.

I also can't stop what I am doing to run to the store. Starting is the hardest part, and I've already pulled out a mixing bowl and flipped to this recipe. If I stop now, I'll just buy a premade pecan pie, slide it into my Nordic Ware pie plate, and lie by omission. The cake is for our neighbors across the street. We're going over for lunch after church tomorrow, and I offered to bring dessert. They wouldn't notice. I have nothing to prove. But I shake my head and pull my all-purpose flour off the shelf.

Cake flour has a lower gluten ratio, making it preferable for spongey things. I measure out two cups of flour and dump them in my bowl. I replace two tablespoons of the flour with equal parts cornstarch, which should improve the ratios. I use my finger to draw a plum line across the spoon, and the starch dusts into the creases of my palm. It feels too smooth, like it shouldn't be tangible.

1 teaspoon baking soda
1 teaspoon baking powder
1/2 teaspoon salt

I learned to bake by watching my mom pull off her wedding rings to knead triple batches of bread or cut biscuits with an inverted sippy cup. She always made do. Every ingredient could be substituted and every recipe could be tweaked. She was always adjusting oven temperatures and baking times to compensate for the three thousand feet of elevation between her California valley hometown and the small Canadian plateau she raised us on. Before I could read, my mom told me that baking powder was the "magic ingredient"; it became my favorite thing to measure out and add to her chocolate chip cookies. In rural Canada, there was only one brand available at the store. It was a brown jar with a yellow label that hadn't changed since the fifties: Magic Baking Powder. The baking powder I have now is the ALDI brand, and even though it cost less than a dollar, I sprinkle it in with a bit of extra reverence.

1 stick of butter
1 cup sugar

I know what to do without reading down the recipe for instructions. When you bake a cake, the wet and dry ingredients are combined separately before being folded together. Sugar is always a wet ingredient by cake laws. (Because of chemistry, I assume.) I warm the butter between my hands before dumping it into the bowl and chasing it with sugar. I lock the mixer and start creaming them together. I rest my head on the cabinet as I absentmindedly scrape down the sides of the bowl.

I know how to bake. But I lie about it all the time. I gush over iced box brownies or cookies that needed less flour and I coo some nonsense.

"Oh, I can't bake. I'm happy to cook, but baking is out of my league!"

"I don't have the time or patience to bake anything!"

I have plenty of time, but I don't bake. In the last year of apparently universal sourdough starters, I don't think I've baked at all. Even the Christmas shortbread cookie mix on top of my pantry remains, though the chocolate drops that were included have long since been poached. Even in the year or two before that, I managed maybe a single pumpkin loaf in the fall or a batch of apple crisps in the summer.

Denying ability or lying about time constraints is easier. I can bake. I might even be good at baking, instinctive. But depression loves to pick at that low-hanging fruit: the quiet, constant hum of my homesickness and nostalgia. So on my best days, it is easier to dismiss activities that remind me of my Aunt Eileen swatting my bum with a towel while insisting that a balanced diet is a cookie in each hand, not three cookies in each. On my worst days I glance around my kitchen and drown in the palpable absence of my sister melting butter to top her knotted bread or my mother grabbing sheet pans out from under me, to "wash as she goes," regardless of whether or not I was done with that pan. So I stay away from the kitchen and the reminders of my mom, and my sister, and my aunts.

1 teaspoon vanilla
2 large eggs

The butter and sugar are pale and fluffy, so I start measuring out vanilla and cracking in eggs. My teal KitchenAid (a wedding gift from Aunt Sheila) beats a rhythm on my uneven countertop as I toss the eggsshells into the trash and splash my hands under the tap.

1 cup buttermilk

I don't have buttermilk either, but I wouldn't buy it anyway. It's a main ingredient in Mom's chocolate cake too. But I don't think I saw actual buttermilk until I was eighteen and I had moved away from home. It's one of the first recipes I learned, and I can see my mom's handwriting on the well-splattered page.

~~1 cup buttermilk~~ 1 tablespoon lemon juice plus milk to make a cup

I squeeze the lemon directly into a measuring spoon and set the rind aside to forget about and throw out later this week. I grab the measuring cup in my left hand and measure out the milk with my hip checking the fridge door and the milk cap between my teeth. I chuck the jug back in the fridge and set my created buttermilk on the counter to curdle a bit.

I used to bake every week. I was a child, but I had my own recipes perfected: mud brownies, homemade peanut butter cups, butterscotch bars. And when I wasn't baking on my own, I was tag-teaming my mom's recipes with Kate. I loved it when we had mashed potatoes for dinner, because it meant that we would bake chocolate cake the next morning (a half cup of unseasoned mashed potatoes is the secret ingredient to a perfectly moist cake). Kate and I tested probably a hundred batches of Dad's cookies until we finally got the right ratio of margarine and flour. I rolled out balls while Kate would flip finished cookies off hot pans and on to paper towels until the whole kitchen counter was tiled with baked goods. For every cookie I rolled, I popped a bite of raw dough in my mouth. What can I say? I was ten. I didn't know about calories and I hadn't gotten salmonella yet.

Preheat oven to 350 degrees.

I fold in the dry ingredients until just mixed and pour it into my greased cake pan. I don't scrape the bowl too thoroughly. After all, any batter left in the bowl is within cake laws to be licked out with a spatula and enjoyed as a pre-cake celebration. And then the cake is in the oven. (Middle rack, thirty-five to forty minutes.)

The slam of the oven door slopes my shoulders down. I was wearing them like earrings and I didn't feel the tension until this moment. I hold the mixing bowl against my chest and lean against the fridge. Damn. I feel . . . settled. The cake is in the oven, and I am twelve again. Years, and still the spots on cookbooks and the rattle of measuring cups and the tang of raw flour on my tongue are all the same.

I forgot it felt like this. The smell of caramelizing sugar and the greasy kiss of butter and the arches of dough in the metal mixing bowl and this resolute satisfaction curling around my chest.

After a decade, I sink right in. (It feels like home.)

I thought my capability had faded with my will. I must have started believing my *I don'ts* and *I can'ts* at some point. But the proof rises in front of me.

Later, I'll make a cream filling, without a recipe (because I don't like the one recommended by *Epicurious*). I'll pull the cake out of the oven and check it with a fork. I'll slice it in half, and frost it, and cover it with fresh strawberries and mint leaves. I'll take a picture and drop it in the family group chat before I bring the cake over to the neighbors. My dad will ask questions about the cream and what I used to stabilize it. My younger sister will pander, "You did it! Good job, you baked something!" (She doesn't remember that I know how.)

And Kate will send me a text that she's proud of me and that cakes are tough for her. It feels different from her. She knows.

But for now, I'm in the kitchen licking a spatula.

years,
and still the spots on cookbooks and the rattle of measuring cups and the tang of raw flour on my tongue are all the same

The Room Is Not Empty

Mark J. Mitchell

She must be here. Her purse hangs there. The air
is bright with flowers. Glasses placed just so.
So perfect, you think it all might break
if you exhale. Stop. Breathe. Now call her name,
soft as some pink blossom. The kitchen knows
her touch. The baking bread tells you where
she stands at this exact time. Cough to show
you'll wait. That you see it all, you're aware
of all she's done—the love, the labor it takes
to offer you a table, simple, not plain.
Today belongs to her homely art. The price
of joy is flour, fire, yeast, and time. Her smile
will decorate the room, will ice that cake,
this feast. There's nothing she needs to explain.

December Gacela

Mark J. Mitchell

Winter blossoms,
that same bright red
as the first kiss
on your mistletoe mouth.
Then, winter

blossoms in rooms
warmed by uncles
and misplaced cousins
whose much longer arms
hug you until
winter

blossoms in their
souls and yours. Then
comes a personal
snowmelt as a laugh
drifts your way
making all
of winter blossom.

Homecoming

Skye Wilson

Pale as snow, and smarter than anyone I know,
her sharp green eyes and auburn hair reflect
the light like ice. She is a shock of sunshine
forcing its way through my darkest days.
She's sliding in the smell of baking cookies,
staggering in my favorite fluffy socks.
She's everyday glimmers of excitement: advent
calendars and almost-settled snow, boozy
hot chocolate that warms me to my soul.
She is icy, pink-cheeked air. With Catriona,
every journey is adventure, the gentle crack
of fire, discovering a new favorite book.
She is cinnamon and citrus, burning candles,
fruit bowls full of chocolate. She is home.

Creation

Skye Wilson

He makes magic with veg and spices,
but on too low a heat for my impatient
mouth—a chef so slow, my new habit
is writing poems as he composes dinner.

Sometimes his hands ease bike chains
to oily quiet, flex wheels back into halos,
replace parts I can't even name. He's filthy
and frowning and emanates the simple joy

of fixing. His brow unfurrows in my arms.
He talks about his work—graphs, coding,
complexity—and asks about mine
with gleaming eyes (he'd never read

a poem before we met). Hair glowing
in the winter sun, a mulled wine
by his elbow as he struggles with a crossword,
ink bleeding through to leave hieroglyphics

on his pale legs—   I should go. Dinner is ready.

Monday Evening

Skye Wilson

I peel carrots in long, careful movements,
pass them to you. You efficiently chop.
I am wearing your jumper and joggies;
you are in your most worn jeans
and a toothpaste-stained T-shirt.

You are warm beside me while sesame oil
kisses the hot pan. I hold you from behind
as you sauté garlic, chili, and ginger;
I go on tiptoe to dab lips onto your neck,
breathe in the scents. I throw in veg;
you stir slowly, other arm around me.
I put out plates.

Soon, we sit, my leg in your lap, voracious.
The spice forces us to pant through burning
mouths—apart from this, silence. Slowly,
then suddenly, we are too satisfied
to eat another bite. I stand, stretch, kiss
your forehead. We take our dishes to the kitchen.

You whip me gently with a towel
while I fill the sink; I splash your face
so your smile shines with bubbles.
You dry the dishes, almost drop a plate,
then, in tandem, we slot perfectly in place.

Hungers

Tomas Baiza

A plate of rice, beans, and my mother's turkey in steaming mole poblano. The tortilla comes whisper-close to the spicy chocolate sauce that's only slightly darker than Brenda Moreno's cinnamon skin.

"Ey, 'pérate. We need to talk."

I roll my eyes and stare at the plate, waiting.

"M'ijo, that's a good dinner, ¿qué no?"

"Yes, Mom." I drop the fork. The flour tortilla is warm in my palm.

"Can you remember a time when you were ever hungry?"

I fold the tortilla between my fingers and close my eyes. Soft and velvety. I shift on my chair. Oh fuck, am I really fondling a tortilla in front of my mother?

"Yeah," I say. "'Orita." *Right now.*

"No. I mean, cuando tenías hambre for real and you couldn't remember the last time you ate and weren't sure the next time you would?"

"Yes I can!" I hate how my voice sounds. I hate being fourteen. I hate that my palm is getting all sweaty and if I keep squirming on my chair my mother will *know.*

Hell is a place where your girlfriend is a floppy, limp tortilla and you have a hard-on at the dinner table.

"No, you can't," she says. "Because you've never felt hunger, have you?"

"No—I mean yes. I'm hungry *right now*, Mom."

"How could you possibly know what hunger is?"

My fingers cling to the tortilla's fading heat. I can't stop thinking about it. Her. "I know, Mom."

I know because Brenda told Nicolás to fuck off and started eating lunch with me, and then Nicolás, Alex, and Martin started calling me marica and bitch and joto, and all of Brenda's girlfriends just giggle at me when I walk by and one of them asked me why I haven't given it to her yet, and Brenda says tomorrow's perfect because her parents are working late.

I want to shout everything, so that she'll know the truth. About me. About what's going to happen.

My mother's almond eyes narrow to slits. "How many times do I have to tell you, m'ijo? You have never known hunger." She runs a hand through thick, blue-black hair. For the first time I notice a faint stripe of gray just above her ear. She sighs and cups my cheek. Her palm is cool against my skin. "Daniel, when I was your age, I ate once a day if I was lucky. Your abuelita would come home from the cannery and maybe your tías and I would get a tin of tomatoes. Maybe some eggs if the chickens were having a good week."

I think about my grandfather's chickens and how I only see them on Thanksgiving or some cousin's quinceañera. It never occurred to me that actual eggs could come from such scrawny things. Brenda's parents don't have chickens. They have a shar-pei.

"Daniel," my mother says, her voice softer now. "Sometimes I think that I failed because you don't understand what it means to truly need."

I plunge the tortilla into the mole. A thin layer has congealed over the cooling sauce and it doesn't look so good anymore. *Need? How do you not understand how bad I need this?* I push the tortilla around the plate, swirling together the rice and beans and guajolote—and then I wonder if they say *guajolote* at Brenda's house or if they just say *turkey* and then I wonder what the regular Spanish and not-Mexican word for *turkey* is and why do I know how to say *dick* and the c-word in Mexican but not the Spanish word for fucking *turkey*?

My mother tears off a piece of tortilla and flicks it in her mouth, her broad teeth quickly turning it to mush. “Dale,” she says. Her eyes are moist and hint at a disappointment I think she was born with. “Go on. Before it goes cold.”

The Scent of Home

Sheryl Guterl

Delicious time,
unexpected pandemic gift.
At home, with nowhere to go,
I search the pantry for amusement.

Flour, yeast, sugar, salt
combine with milk,
to texture of thick mud.
My hands dig into soft mush;

push, pull, push, pull.
Softness, resilience result.
Alchemy begins.
Mixture balloons.

Punch down, rise again,
roll, shape, admire
smooth mounds rest in pans
like breasts in a bra.

Inflate once more, then
bake till golden loaves
scent the house and create home.
Butter melts into delicious slice.

Delicious

Sheryl Guterl

Like spaghetti
coiled in a bowl,
our conversations
loop and curve.

His clever mind untwists
hidden meanings,
subtle shadings,
layers of flavor.

A spicy turn
brings a twinkle,
then a giggle, until
we are laughing.

Under scoops of verbal gravy
on our mashed conversation
lies wisdom; often we have
different points of view.

Eschewing the sourness of
aging joints, rancid politics,
and difficult people,
all too bitter to swallow,

we choose sweet dreams,
or catch sunlight's
delight in cactus flower
the color of lemon ice,

cool jazz smooth as
chocolate pudding,
framed watercolor subtle
as saffron in rice.

our conversations
loop

and curve

Inheritance

Sheryl Guterl

Her blue eyes were a shade lighter,
but my veined arthritic fingers
look just like hers.

"Be careful!" comes out of my mouth
automatically in my mother's voice
when someone leaves the house.

My need for visual order likely
stems from my mother, for whom
cleanliness was above godliness.

But today I know that my
best inheritance is a love of
brown, bubbly baked beans.

For these, there is no recipe,
but I remember watching Mother make them.
Rinse canned baked beans,

add ketchup, molasses, onions,
Worcestershire sauce, brown sugar,
in unmeasured, instinctual amounts.

Scoop into crockery, lay slices of bacon
on top, then bake low and slow
for hours of sweet-pungent aroma.

I have a stack of her recipes,
copied onto note cards
in her Palmer Method handwriting—

apple crisp, potato salad,
dozens of chicken casseroles,
and tomato aspic.

Each reads like a novel
when memories
are stirred into the ingredients.

when memories
are stirred into
the ingredients

The Joys of an Old Cookery Book

Alex Grehy

Two events of small significance took place in 1963: the Good Housekeeping Institute reprinted its cookery book, and I was born.

In a rural Welsh village, a woman takes her brand-new copy of the *Good Housekeeping Cookery Book* from her shopping bag. I imagine her sitting at her kitchen table, sipping a cup of tea as she flicks through its six hundred pages. The book is luxurious—a glossy dust jacket wrapped around sturdy dove-gray boards, which are embossed with the title in gold lettering. The book has vivid color photographs of immaculately presented dishes, along with lavishly illustrated section headers. At the back of the book there are three blank pages headed "For Additional Recipes."

Over the next eighteen years, the woman cherishes the book, at some point replacing the dust jacket with a neatly folded cover made of floral pastel wallpaper. Then, I suspect, she died. The book ended up in a charity shop where my mother found it in 1981.

I've been baking all my life. As a girl I helped my grandmother in the kitchen. By the time I was eleven, the great responsibility of making the family's Christmas cake fell into my willing hands.

As I approached my eighteenth birthday, it became evident that I would be more clever than beautiful. My family concluded that the only way I was going to make friends at university, and lure a husband, was through cookery. On the morning of my coming of age, I unwrapped presents that included icing spatulas, earthenware mixing bowls, baking tins, and this precious secondhand copy of the *Good Housekeeping Cookery Book*, published in the year of my birth.

Forty years later, I still treasure the book. It predates food processors and the availability of prepared ingredients.

The recipe for apple strudel involves making filo pastry from flour, eggs, and warm water, placing the dough on a floured cloth the size of your kitchen table and pulling the pastry until it is paper thin. It has recipes for making fudge, mint humbugs, and hard candies. It assumes an abundance of ingredients and no shortage of skills as you cream, knead, and mix your way from first principles to a table laden with delicious homemade food.

Modern staples, like spaghetti Bolognese, are tucked into a slim chapter titled "Continental Recipes." Travel to Europe, even from the UK, was then a treat for the elite—to this day, my mother has never been abroad. To quote the cookbook: "Even those who have little chance of traveling are becoming interested in foreign food, and many a housewife finds it rekindles her zest for cooking if she includes an occasional continental dish in the menu."

Yet, for me, the most magical pages are those headed "For Additional Recipes." The previous owner has lovingly written a few of her own recipes in looped, confident handwriting. I imagine her floury hands reaching to me across the years. I wonder who she was. Would we have enjoyed cooking together? I have no doubt that she never imagined these recipes would become a legacy. When I read them, I had a vision that one day I might hand the book over to another cook, so I added a few more recipes in my own crabbed handwriting.

In 2012, disaster struck. My mischievous dogs got hold of the cookery book while I was out and used it as a chew toy. Luckily, with the help of some sticky tape, it survived, though the bottom corner of the index pages was shredded to confetti. The book is still usable, but I grieved as I became convinced that there was no hope of it ever being passed on to another generation of cooks in its ruined state.

But will the next generation even use cookery books? I have moved on, frequently using the internet to search for recipes. I record my adventures in cooking on social media. Yet I still keep my *Good Housekeeping Cookery Book* for its authenticity. If you need a recipe for mincemeat or marmalade or crumpets—for anything that is simpler to buy prepared than make, then this is THE cookbook.

As I write this, I feel a great surge of love for my tattered fifty-eight-year-old cookbook, currently sitting next to my laptop. I wonder whether I should try again to restore its integrity with more sticky tape and a new cover made from wallpaper. Would anyone want a vintage cookbook, bearing the marks of a busy life in the kitchen? There are still a few spaces for another generation of recipes.

My *Good Housekeeping Cookery Book* from 1963 is not a museum piece. I refer to it frequently, but there is a very particular ritual that I want to share—the ritual of Stir-Up Sunday.

Stir-Up Sunday falls in November, a week before Advent Sunday, and is the traditional day for making Christmas pudding. Being a secular household, I had always believed that the name "Stir-Up Sunday" referred to the tradition of every member of the household taking a turn to stir the pudding mixture and making a wish. However, its true origin is the prayer "Stir up, we beseech thee, O Lord, the wills of thy faithful people," the litany for the Sunday before Advent as listed in the Book of Common Prayer.

In various guises, people have included the pudding in their Christmas feasting for six hundred years or more. In that time it has gathered its own legends—ideally it should have thirteen ingredients, one each for Jesus and the twelve apostles; old silver sixpenny pieces stirred into the mixture bestowed good fortune on anyone lucky enough to find one in their slice of pudding.

But the ever-practical *Good Housekeeping Cookery Book* ignores the pudding's mythical status and just lists the ingredients and methodology for making this rich, sweet, fruity, spicy steamed suet dessert. It is simple to make, but with at least thirteen ingredients, five hours cooking in a steamer, and four weeks in storage with weekly dousings of brandy, I can see why a homogenized plastic basin that has been on sale in the supermarket since Halloween might appeal. Not in my house!

I've been making my own Christmas puddings on Stir-Up Sunday forever, but around twenty years ago I invited a friend to join me in the making. Word got around, and now Stir-Up Sunday has become a major event in our social calendar. I usually have fifteen or more people joining in to make puddings in my kitchen, followed by a huge lunch and merriment. The puddings themselves are very popular, and I now make around thirty puddings every year, which I ship all over the world in exchange for donations to charity.

But back to my house on what is usually the last Sunday in November, when the days are short, and the last few leaves are clinging to the oak tree that grows in my garden. The air is full of birdsong as the robins and blue tits flock to the bird feeders, having long since eaten their way through the fruit in my orchard. Although there is a chill in the air, my kitchen is warm and smells of brandy. The secret of a good Christmas pudding is soaking the dried fruit overnight in a generous amount of spirit—usually brandy, but I favor rum. This makes the fruit plump and juicy, and helps to preserve the pudding in storage. The aroma of the spirit-infused fruit is intoxicating.

On the windowsill of my kitchen, bags and jars of dry ingredients are neatly laid out, along with an array of spoons, mixing bowls, and two antique scales, their brass weighing pans and battered weights gleaming. The big table in the center of the room is laid with everyone's individual recipes and instructions, along with spare pudding basins and clean cotton aprons. I enjoy this moment of calm when everything is neat and tidy.

At 11 a.m., the Stirrers arrive—friends and family all eager to mix their puddings. Soon the house is filled with laughter and the air is full of flying flour and spices. Despite my meticulously prepared instruction sheets, there is always a degree of mayhem as the Stirrers scramble to gather their ingredients and get stirring. There is hot competition to be the first to finish. It's my job, as referee, to make sure that their haste doesn't lead to ingredients being omitted or salt being substituted for sugar!

By 12:30 p.m. it seems that there may be more flour on the floor than in the mixing bowls, and every utensil in the kitchen is covered in pudding mixture. But then, suddenly, it's time for the last stir, when everyone makes a wish, and the mixture is spooned into pudding basins and carefully covered with greaseproof paper ready for steaming. Everyone labels their pudding and sets them aside. Steaming a small pudding takes around three hours, so that's done in the comfort of their own homes. My friends and family then diligently clean up, incentivized by the aroma of the roast dinner that I've been preparing while they've been stirring.

We spend the afternoon eating and chatting, buoyed by the rich smells of spices and spirits. We chew over the year's events and look forward to Christmas Day, when our puddings will be the centerpiece of the dessert table. The lights will be turned down low and flaming brandy poured over the pudding. The pure blue flames will flicker over its deep bronze surface, filling the air with soft light and the warm fragrance of toasted sugar and spice.

By 6 p.m. on Stir-Up Sunday, the Stirrers will have wandered home, and I'll get the steamer out and cook the pudding I prepared earlier.

Last year, the pandemic lockdown meant that we were not allowed to gather in person for Stir-Up Sunday. I thought we'd have to abandon our lovely ritual, but the Stirrers wailed so loudly I had to find a way. As with so many pursuits, technology provided the answer.

The Stirrers always choose their own combination of fruit, spices, and spirits in accordance with their preferences. They let me know in advance, and I organize the ingredients, as there are economies of scale in buying them centrally. 2020 was no different, except this time I gathered, weighed, and packaged the ingredients, along with the instructions, and sent them to the Stirrers by courier.

On the day itself, we set up a Zoom call and at 11 a.m. on the Sunday before Advent, we mixed our puddings together with exactly the same amount of laughter and mayhem, but considerably less flour on my kitchen floor. Texts and WhatsApp messages flew through the ether as Stirrers queried the directions. Mixing bowls were held up to cameras for me to check whether they'd achieved the perfect soft dropping consistency in their final mixtures. The joy of this new approach was that many more Stirrers could join in the fun as it's certain that they would never have all fitted into my kitchen at the same time. Which is a dilemma, as they all want to join in Stir-Up Sunday in person this year. I'm sure we'll find a way. This ritual has transcended every challenge through the ages, and I know it will continue to do so.

Read Alex Grehy's Christmas Pudding Recipe online at capsulestories.com/christmas-pudding-recipe

Christmas Cookies

C. T. Holte

Most of the stars and trees
were recognizable as such.
Some of the gingerbread men required imagination:
Mutants? Too much flour? No matter;
we remembered the concept of "family cookies."

We mourned the loss of cookie cutters past,
the treasured shapes abandoned
during our various transitions
along with the spare spatulas
deemed redundant for a single baker.

But what we had was good enough and more.
We smiled at thoughts of times
as kitchen helpers in our youth,
and our own children helping us in turn,
wondered if the tradition held in their new homes.

As the kitchen filled with the season's smells,
we marveled at the blessing of these bakers:
the goodness of the baked,
the magic blending of ingredients
in the old bowls and in our new lives together.

Honey

C. T. Holte

I lick a dribble of honey
from between my fingers,
note the little blob on my placemat,
capture a new leak with my knife
before it oozes off my toast
and onto my plate.

Over this honey-infused life
I wonder how many units—
dabs, globs, spoonfuls, pounds—
I have unthinkingly squandered,
how many bee-hours I have devalued
with overspreading, sloppy eating,
lack of attention to the slow flow
toward an available low point.

Perhaps honey is sentient after all,
driven by the urge
to reject toast, plates, those cute
little wooden honey-dipper things,
escape the eager mouths of breakfasters,
and return to its borning blossoms.

Too much philosophy, too little coffee!
I lick another attempted escape
from another sticky finger,
take another honeyed bite of toast
pour myself a second cup of French roast.

Evolution

C. T. Holte

Fat was a solution then,
not a problem:
my grandmother's miracles
employed bacon fat and lard.
Bacon was a breakfast necessity,
with the bonus of grease
to fry the breakfast eggs
and the diced potatoes for dinner.
Lard ruled the baking.

Angels would float earthward
when Grandma's oven door opened,
hovering outside the kitchen window
to inhale the aromas of her apple pies,
while we hovered inside,
hoping to be blessed
with an afternoon treat of leftover dough
sprinkled with cinnamon and sugar
and baked to a heavenly golden brown.

My parents graduated to the big city
and a modern kitchen: piped-in gas;
running water, not a bucket and dipper;
hot water from the tap, no big pot
simmering constantly on the back burner
as at Grandma's Grandpa-built bungalow.

But there was no quid pro quo:
change does not guarantee progress.

Angels will have nothing to do with Crisco,
nor could they relate to the cans and packages
from which my mother's pies emerged.
Grandma, like an angel, had no comment.

Old memories resonate as we relearn
what grandmas knew: fresh from scratch is better,
and even more better with butter;
spoiling a kid's appetite is not a crime.

I long for the day when science will verify
what the angels have always known:
bacon and lard are spiritual foods.

old memories resonate
as we relearn what
grandmas knew

Giving Thanks

C. T. Holte

Similar turkey: fresh, not frozen.
Similar potatoes, but missing an ingredient:
your company potatoes are fine,
but Grandma Lois knew spuds need butter.

Beans without the mushroom soup
or those crispy fried onions
threaten the transition a bit;
your oyster dressing atones in part.

The king of gravy (me!) stirs once more:
drippings in the roux bring color,
butter and brandy richen,
sage and simmer provide finesse.

Different house, blended families,
similar but different histories,
same prayers, new love and thankfulness.
And big bowls of everything.

It's Never the Knife's Fault

Larry Griggs

Content warning: racism, police encounter

Mac and cheese is as simple a meal as it can get. It's packed with flavor in every cheesy bite. The dish is also playful as it leaves a little string of cheese on your chin. No one will say, "Hey, you got some cheese on your chin." No, they will nod and whisper, "Leave it." It's a fact that food and love are scientifically the same—they release the same chemical reaction in our brains. When I think of love, I think of home, and when I think of home, I think of mac and cheese. In a *Forrest Gump* interpretation, macaroni and cheese can be baked, stovetop, put in grilled cheese, used on a burger, etc. The Cheesecake Factory has fried mac and cheese balls. Best thing ever. Macaroni and cheese is more than a dish, it is a culture, and as a culture it can have different connotations.

As history goes, it was said that the classic American mac and cheese returned with Thomas Jefferson to America after his vacation in Italy. Jefferson brought back a pasta machine from Italy and along with it a mac and cheese recipe. That's right, people, the man who initiated the Trail of Tears helped bring America mac and cheese. And here I used to think that some white people didn't eat the stuff.

The first time I went to a white household to eat dinner was for my girlfriend Laura's family's Thanksgiving dinner. We'd been dating for a few months. Her family celebrated every year at Laura's aunt's house, who was known to be a very religious person. Her Aunt Tammy only wore skirts and believed only sinners watched television. Aunt Tammy's house was a quaint home, and to my surprise, the food was ready when we arrived. Usually in my household, the host would say a certain time, but when you arrived the food would still be cooking, and dinner wouldn't start until two hours later. After introductions, the "Oh, he's Black," we started making our way into the kitchen to fix our plates. I filled my plate with turkey, ham, mashed potatoes, then there was a disturbance in the Force. I began searching through the containers and pans on the kitchen counter. I looked in the oven and in the refrigerator. Panic began to settle in.

"What's he looking for, Laura?" they asked. Laura came over and put an arm around my waist.

"What are you looking for?" she asked.

I turned toward her with frantic eyes. "Where's the mac and cheese?"

There wasn't any confusion in the room. I think they might have laughed a little. I lifted the tin foil off a pan that held something that resembled mac and cheese but was informed that it was corn pudding.

"Mac and cheese?" Laura's uncle Dave said. He said the words as if they were foreign. "We don't have none of that."

No mac and cheese? I'd never had a family dinner without mac and cheese. It felt like a friend had died, and I had forgotten and asked for them anyway. I sat down with my plate next to Laura, and after we said grace, I began to eat my incomplete meal. Laura's aunt must have seen my disappointment. She excused herself and went into the kitchen. A while later she said that there was some macaroni and cheese ready for me. I frowned when I saw it. In a Tupperware container sat something that resembled a glob of dried yellow glue, and next to it sat the open carcass of processed cheddar.

"You get your macaroni fix?" she asked as I returned to the table with a small portion.

Barely able to swallow it, I nodded. Later, when everyone was finished eating, I sent a photo of the atrocity in the kitchen to my best friend Kelly, who had graduated from culinary school the previous year.

He texted a few moments later: *Have your stomach pumped. IMMEDIATELY.* There wasn't an LOL at the end. He was serious. On the ride home after the meal, Laura asked how the dinner was.

"Do white people not eat mac and cheese?" I was serious.

"Don't be racist," she said jokingly.

No Veggies Allowed in Mac and Cheese. Repeat Offenders Will Be Kicked Out of the Family.

Serves eight and the occasional Black joke.

Instructions

1. Bring water to a boil in a medium saucepan. Season with salt.
2. Once water is boiling, stir in macaroni. Cook for 10–12 minutes, stirring occasionally or until al dente.
3. Drain the noodles.
4. Pick up the white packet of . . . cheese? Hold it to the light. Mutter, "What the hell is this?" Shrug. Open it and dump hastily in the pot with the macaroni. Add milk. Stir.
5. Proceed to destroy your stomach.
6. Throw the whole family away.

Christmas dinner was held at my mother's house. She asked me to bring Laura, and when we arrived she proceeded to show every embarrassing feature of my childhood.

There were pictures of me in a dress and when I had slipped and broken my ankle. (Thanks, Mom.) My brother, who had recently been divorced, brought his new girlfriend. This was how it was with him: if you spent a night in jail, he got put on the FBI's most wanted list. If you had a cold, he had Ebola. If you'd dodged one bullet, he'd dodged five and caught one with his teeth. Blindfolded. His girlfriend Riley was also white, blonde and big-boned. She gave everyone a hug in succession starting with my mom first. When she got to me I looked at her and tried to sound polite.

"I don't do hugs."

My mother had moved recently, and her new home wasn't as big as the house that we'd grown up in. She told us as she finished setting the table since it was just her that she didn't need the extra space. As I looked around the two-bedroom house, I felt as though that statement was completely inaccurate. The paintings on the walls were crammed like sardines. When Mom went to get the silverware, my brother told us that she'd lost the house. She gathered us in the dining room where we sat cramped around a table that took up the majority of the room. After sliding and reaching over people's arms and torsos, we were able to eat. As a college student, it had been a while since I had had some good food. The table was full of dishes: turkey, golden brown, and deep fried turkey, honey-glazed country ham, collard greens, macaroni and cheese, green beans, mashed potatoes, sweet potatoes mashed and covered with marshmallows, corn, cornbread, my mom's famous sweet rolls, potato salad, cranberry sauce from the can, and for dessert something called a bourbon candy apple cheesecake. I was already done with one plate and was starting on another when the unthinkable happened.

Riley took a bite and said loudly, "This mac and cheese is nasty."

I'm pretty sure time froze. Silence flooded the house like a fog. Even the baby who was crying to be breastfed froze mid-scream.

"Everything else is good, the mac and cheese is just nasty."

She said it again! Our eyes drifted to where my mother sat at the head of the table. Her eyes narrowed, and my brother's eyes closed and his mouth moved silently in prayer. After a moment, she continued to eat, and time unfroze.

There are certain rules when it comes to eating mac and cheese in a Black home: First, if it is bad, you nibble the good parts (these are indicated by the globs of melted cheese), and when you go get seconds, you discreetly dump it in the trash and place a napkin over it. Second, you never ever tell the cook that it was bad.

In Black culture, macaroni and cheese is the highest culinary honor. Who makes it, how it's made, and who's allowed to bring it to a dinner involves tests, approval from Obama, and extreme tacit understanding. The person who makes the mac and cheese is held in high esteem. It is their burden—no, their privilege—to ensure that the dynamic of the family stays intact. Because mac and cheese maintains the status quo, and the answer to the question "Who made this?" is something to be earned. You have to go on a hero's quest and be blessed by Jesus, Allah, the Virgin Mother, and Buddha just to boil the macaroni noodles. Just pull out a box of Kraft? That's the same as punching a hole through your grandma's heart.

After the dinner as Riley and my brother were leaving, she hugged my mother again. My mother hugged her. After Riley left, my mother turned to me and said, "I don't like that bitch."

Mama PG's Southern Home Cooking

Riley D., from Guest Comment, says:
Had dinner with my new man, y'all. Something for everyone. Service was awesome, and Mama PG was very accommodating. Mac and cheese needs work tho. Will definitely be back!

Valeria S., from Guest Comment, says:
Is she trying to get stabbed? Yo, Anthony, you need to get ya girl, bruh.

Anthony G., from Guest Comment, says:
Lord, if I can just make it through another dinner without any more problems, that would be great!

In a commercial Kendall Jenner gave a cop a Pepsi. Just a simple gesture, but it caused an uproar in the Black Lives Matter community. The ad was ridiculed and criticized for being insensitive and implausible—it seemed that Pepsi was trying to say their product could cure years of racism and racial profiling. Even then I laughed at the absurdity and laughed even harder when the internet made memes about the incident. Later, I wondered if one act of communion or even the symbol of the olive branch could sway a person's opinion. A different outcome, but the same logic I suppose.

I wrecked my car in the summer of 2015, and that summer I worked at a grocery store. After I got off one day, I bought a box of macaroni and walked behind the store to avoid my coworkers asking me if I needed a ride home. I stuck to the sidewalk away from the road and followed it toward the Greenbelt Trail. My thoughts were interrupted when I saw the dog running from the stoop of a home. It was a small dog, no bigger than the size of my cat, but the way it ran after me caused me to almost drop my bag of macaroni and run like Usain Bolt. I heard the paws click on the sidewalk as I ran, the rumble between growl and bark. I made it to the stop sign, out of breath and dripping with sweat when I realized it no longer chased me. It must have veered off without me noticing it. I straightened my sweaty shirt and was about to walk again when I locked eyes with a truck. I waited. I had to cross the street. The truck didn't budge; we were locked in a fierce staring contest until seconds later four bicycle cops screeched to a stop. Two cop cars pulled on the curb, cutting off every possible exit. I was surrounded. I was reminded of a drug bust that I had seen on TV the night before. I looked around, searching for whatever criminal the police were looking for, and then it dawned on me. That person they were after was *me*. The man in the truck got out first. He was a stout, short man with brown hair that looked like grass.

If I had stopped the officers there and made the mac and cheese for them, would it change their minds about the color of people's skin?

"Just eat it," I would plead, arms outstretched, showcasing the melted cheese overflowing, bubbling, and steaming. This would be my olive branch, my favorite food and my own Novocain to the horrors of this world. All the differences in our lives are mere surface details compared to food and what it could accomplish in our world. One bite of mac and cheese and they'd understand my message of passion, kinship, and generosity. They'd taste the value of community, the promise that food symbolizes. Because what is food if not an expression of love? In this day and age the cops refuse, they will look at my offering with disdain, violating the sanctity of communion, and I in return end up on the news as another unarmed Black male gunned down by the police. However, the goal was not to win the argument, but to make it home.

"Do you mind if I search you?" the officer asked.

I complied and raised my arms, which might have looked funny considering the box of macaroni in a bag.

"A woman said that she saw you running. There was a robbery a few days back, so she called the police. You want to tell us why you were running?"

I laughed at the absurdity. "Oh, there was a dog."

"A dog?" one of the bike cops asked.

I was beginning to feel claustrophobic from all the bodies that closed in on me. I felt in a matter of seconds I would be possessed and become one of them like in the third *Matrix* movie.

"What kind of dog?"

"I don't know, a small one."

"You ran from a small dog?" he questioned, eyebrows raised.

I laughed again, this time out of nervousness. "Yeah, you see a dog, you run from it."

"Where you coming from?"

I was beginning to feel irritated and I could feel the sweat forming on my forehead because of the heat. I glanced at the work shirt that clearly indicated my place of employment still draped over my arm.

"I just got off work."

After verifying that I was indeed coming from work, the officer gave me a ride home: in the back, like a criminal. The space was cramped. I barely had room to stretch out my legs. I looked out the window at the nice houses that I couldn't imagine affording and now was banned from. Between us was the partition that separated prestige and criminal.

My mother called later that night. She said one of her friends had seen me as they drove by, and she wanted to make sure that I was still alive.

"Christ, David, you already have one criminal trespassing charge," she said.

My mother was referring to another incident, same shit, different day. Like all mothers, she asked me what I was making for dinner. I looked at the box of macaroni still in the crumpled bag on the kitchen table where I'd left it when I walked in the door. It was now bent, dirt had gotten on it. Tainted. I tossed it in the trash.

"Chinese," I tell her.

Big Momma P's Famous Fixer Elixir Mac and Cheese

Ingredients

3 cups macaroni, uncooked
2 eggs
1/2 cup heavy cream
1 1/2 cups milk
Salt and pepper
A lot of shredded cheese, like three bags, maybe more (I like Colby Jack, but choose whatever)

Instructions

1. Preheat oven to 350 degrees.
2. Cook your macaroni noodles according to the box, just don't overcook! Please, this is

crucial. Drain, and then put back into the pan.

3. Combine the milk, heavy cream, eggs, and at least five cups of cheese. Mix that shit. Pour it into the macaroni already cooked into the pan.

4. Add salt and pepper. Dash of garlic powder. Got some paprika? Boy! Sprinkle that in too, baby. The most important thing I can tell you today is that everything needs seasoning. High blood pressure? We're here for a good time, not a long time.

5. Mix.

6. Pour everything into the baking dish. Make sure the ingredients are evenly distributed. Sprinkle some more cheese on top, then pop it in the oven for 45 minutes, or until the top layer is light brown.

7. Eat and enjoy while it lasts. Tomorrow waits for no one.

I would like to say that macaroni and cheese comes out perfect every time. That the cheese doesn't get congealed, or when you add too much heavy cream or milk it doesn't get soupy. There's a quote by Daniel Boulud that goes, "Remember, it is never the knife's fault." The knife can destroy or help you heal. In my case, the choice to dwell on being racially profiled rested in my hilt. A person is responsible for their actions, their own knives. And as for mac and cheese, it's just a placebo, a kiss from your mother. It can't heal the wounds, but it can alleviate the pain.

I try to visit my mother once a week. She is sixty now, and legally blind, so they say. Whenever she gives me money she can still tell a hundred bill from a dollar. During the week, she babysits my sister's two children even though they give her a hard time. I play with the oldest one, he's four going on thirty-two, and my mom and I talk about the television show *Chopped* and about how people with the sob stories always seem to win.

"You know, I have never seen anyone on the show make mac and cheese," I say.

We then go about our techniques, and when I tell her how I make my own mac and cheese, she looks at me with a weird expression on her face. She gets up and slaps me lightly against the back of the head.

"Boy, you've been making it wrong!"

Recipe for Pasta Figolé at Christmas

Nicole Farmer

Dice the onions.
sing
Sliver the garlic.
hum
Pour the olive oil into the sauté pan.
tap your foot
Wash, dry, and cut the parsley with scissors.
look at that sunshine
Open large cans of Italian whole tomatoes.
turn up Dr. John to volume ten
Chop carrots, celery, and kale.
spin around, ma chère
Run water into the biggest pot you got for boiling the pasta.
love that zydeco, baby
Add a dash of salt when the water boils.
feet got to move
Open six to eight cans of cannellini beans, rinse and drain.
kick off your shoes
Heat the oil and sauté onions, garlic, and red pepper flakes.
hips start to gyrate
Dump in tomatoes and MASH them.
brush hair out of eyes
Splash of wine to taste.
"Quitters never win,
16 oz. chicken stock upended.
and a winner don't never quit."
Scrape in all those vegetables from the chopping board.
clap your hands

More wine!
snap your fingers
Add beans.
two-step, baby
Salt and pepper to taste.
pop that dish towel
Add secret ingredient last: plenty of sage, I mean plenty.
Yes, darlin', my babies are coming home!

Cover and simmer.

Yes, darlin', my babies are coming home!

Curry Pots and Raspberry Bins

Maggi McGettigan

We are cleaning out my mother's house, trying to decide what things are important enough to keep. It is a hard task. She is moving to a nursing home where she will only have one small room, certainly not enough for ninety years of collecting. And who are we, my sister and I, to decide what goes with her, what goes with us, and what goes to Goodwill? We are objects too, we are part of her collections. We didn't stop by often enough after Dad died, we didn't call to check in each night, we didn't offer to move in or have her come to us.

"Look," Lisa says, and holds up a heavy pot stained with years of use. Not clean enough to donate. Not small enough to send.

"Curry pot," we say together, and smile. Of course there were other things cooked in it, but that was Mom's curry pot. When the weather turned cold and the days short, we would come home to the smell of a curry that had been stewing all day. It was comfort, it was love. Her friends begged for the recipe, but it changed all the time, it wasn't something she could write down. "You have to feel it," she would say. "Sometimes potatoes, sometimes not. Depends." Her friends would look at each other and roll their eyes, thinking she was holding back. But that was always how she cooked.

The first Christmas without Dad was the first without curry. Usually it sat on the stove all day, warming the house from the kitchen out. Coming in from the cold, the smell was like warmth itself. To have Christmas without it marked a period of coldness in our lives, one without Dad to be the buffer in arguments, without his ability to lighten the mood. We visited less and less. I almost forgot about the curry.

Lisa puts the pot in the growing pile of not sure yet and goes back into the kitchen. I fold clothes Mom hadn't worn in years.

"Oh my God, Cath," I hear after a while, so I go into the kitchen. Pots, pans, dish towels, plates, and mugs are spread in a sort of chaotic organization. Lisa's head and upper body are hidden inside a lower cabinet. She reemerges holding a stack of mismatched Tupperware bowls and bins. Almost all of them are stained with shades of red and pink.

Suddenly I am ten, crawling behind Lisa under a canopy of thorny branches, hunting for raspberries. It is hot and my skin is sticky with sweat and dirt and scrapes. But I am so happy. Lisa has started biking to town with friends on these long summer days, a privilege I am too young for, and I am always left out. But now she is with me all day, she is my playmate again, and we are on an adventure. We fill our Tupperware bowls to the brim, even after eating the same weight ourselves. When we go back, Mom will make a raspberry sauce that we pour over ice cream at night and waffles in the morning.

A few years ago, I took my own kids raspberry picking at a local farm and tried to recreate the sauce. Something was off, but they ate it anyway. I meant to ask Mom for help, but then the calm of summer became the chaos of back to school, and the project slipped from my mind.

I go home and try to make curry for my kids. It doesn't smell quite the same, but the kitchen feels warm, like home. The kids don't love it. But then I think, I make a damn good grilled cheese. It's not fancy, it's no different than the one we can get at the diner, but they love it. When they are in college and they miss me but don't know how to say it, they might say, I miss your grilled cheese. And we will laugh because it's so easy. But it's mine, and they miss it.

This week, I'll visit Mom and ask her for the curry recipe. I know she will say it's different every time, it's not something you can write down, you have to feel it. But I think she will be happy that I asked and to know that I miss it.

it's not something you can write
down, you have to feel it

Arepas at Night

Laine Derr

I sit, keeping her company
while the dough forms, music
soft enough to hear the words
we do not speak, evening walks
within desert willow, tourists
hoping parking lots are near—
night surrounds them, and us,
heart to your heart, eyes
to your eyes, a flowering tree,
slow-growing, is the only tremor.

Soft Meringue Kisses

Fran Fernández Arce

I steal pieces, glances of my abuelita's
cabinets to assemble an exhibition
of who she is today. Nectarine sweetness,

rose water drops, half-empty bottles
pungent with shades of red
and mauve, saltwater-infused shards of

leftover glass, edges once softened
by gentle lappings of the sea. When she forgets
how my face makes for the sounds

in my name, I let her nightgowns slide
down the stairs like cascading
silhouettes, crumbled naphthalene flakes

rising from the folds. I could make
a patchwork from tatters and cloths. A new
bed cover, curtains, and cushions, stitches

brought together by lavender seeds and deep
sugary cloves. I would call the exhibition
by her name, each installation a mirror

slightly distorted around the center, a faint
layer of icing sugar across the edges,
asking her to remember how she used to

bake cakes from scratch. Soft meringue
kisses, blistering cherry bombs, dulce de leche
and pineapple layers of warmth.

Homemade Magic

Joshua Flores

Heady sweetness permeates the air around me. It's not the intoxicating scent of chocolate heated in simmering milk, nor the hypnotic smell of baking cookies. The aroma comes from steamed corn leaves spiced with heat-congealed maíz encrusting a savory pork mole.

¡Josué! ¡Todavía no! Wait. They need to cool a little.

Mami's voice. She isn't standing over the giant black pot with her tongs ready to slap at my hand lest I dare try to snake out a prize. But I hear her voice anyway.

I pause, closing my eyes, remembering every Christmas and every slapping away of my hand. In my memories, she is vibrant, healthy, smiling. Alive.

Mi hijo, be careful! ¡Esta caliente! Pour it in the masa slowly. There. Stop. Good.

My mind paints her, back arched over willingly, readily. Her hands massaged the masa, soothing the hot melted pork lard into the dough, coerced it to merge with the grains, to smooth out the sharpness. The air in the kitchen is a battlefield of fragrances: cooking pork, simmering mole sauce, soaking corn leaves in hot water to make them supple—malleable.

Así. Yes, just like that. Smooth the masa over the leaf with the back of the spoon. Not too thick. Bueno.

I look up, half expecting to see her sitting at the table with my sisters. An assembly line creating magic born of love and laughter, stories being told, people remembered.

Mami is missing. The laughter, the stories, and my sisters are there. But she is not. Is the magic still there? The stories are of her. They will be enough. They have to be.

I join the table and pick up one of the prepared yellow husks filled to almost overflowing, waiting to be wrapped.

Ahora, bend the right side to the center. Yes, left side now, just over the right side. Muy bien.

It is added to a growing mountain, waiting to be carefully placed into the pot that has been with us for over half a century. She treasured that pot. Kept it away to be used only to make tamales, posole, and menudo. Time seasoned it, made it more perfect so that each batch of food it made came out even better than before.

One person per job. Nadamás. Too many will make it not work. The tamales will fall apart and not cook right.

For fifty-four years Mami had a hand in every tamal made in her kitchen. Even if her body didn't let her do more than give instructions to my sisters in a soft wheezing whisper during the last decade, they were still blessed by her. My eyes close again.

Mira, put each tamal with its open side pointed toward the center, remember to only go in a circle, pressing around the side of the cazuela. There has to be a pozo, a well in the middle so the steam may perform its magic.

My sisters take turns in lining the old pot with their gifts of love, chattering about what is the right way and how did Mami tell us to do it and how mad she would get if they got it wrong. They laugh until they remember Mami isn't there to get mad anymore and they stop. The silence speaks of their wishing it was not so. My wish joins theirs.

Pick up the pot and put it on the stove. Be careful not to drop it. Okay. Okay.

My sisters don't have to say a word, they just look at me. Nodding, I stand, form a small triangle with my legs to the floor, bend down with my knees. They complain with loud cracking. My sisters laugh. "Old man," they tease. I shrug. I lift the pot. It is somehow heavier than it has ever been. Maybe I'm old. Or maybe I lifted more than just the pot?

Josué, I need the cazuela back on the table. Watch it, it's hot and heavy. That's it.

The pot sits on the flame for an hour or so while we regrow the mountain of tamales and add a twin. One of my sisters goes home to get her own cazuela, fills it up, and sets it to steam. The other pot is removed. I lift the lid, and the steam rushes out in a cloud of perfumes and heat. My hand reaches inside. *Slap!* My youngest sister has Mami's tongs, and they sting just the same. "Wait. Why do you need these to remind you every year?" I laugh. She joins me, but it is Mami's laugh I hear. It feels right.

Go back to work. These won't make themselves! ¡Ándale!

The stories continue as do the making and cooking for hours. The mountains of uncooked presents loaded with love-magic transform into giant bowls and containers full of cooked joy. As they cool down, so does our grief. Mami is with us, in that kitchen, sitting at the table, scolding us as we pick out every small mistake we made, and then smiling. Her laugh is musical and honest, and we know she is happy.

Now you can have one, mi hijo. Well, more than one. You must eat. You are a growing boy.

I stare at the plate of orange-red corn-leaf packets. They look just like Mami's. They smell just like Mami's. They are cooked just like she made them. But will the magic be there? I peel one and place its contents on another plate. I say a prayer. For it. For Mami. For me. For the magic.

Mami is home.

Spices

Agnieszka Filipek

smelling freshly ground pepper
I'm back again in my parents' kitchen
my mother grinding black pepper
in the old pepper mill before dinner

and smelling cinnamon I'm back
again watching my grandmother
on a wooden stool chopping apples
we gathered in the garden for an apple pie

as I was growing she somehow was getting smaller
maybe so she could fit inside my heart
and I could carry her with me
after she had gone

Another Day

Agnieszka Filipek

You're nowhere I look.
I hope you're satisfied.
I'm dressed uncomfortably
in ironed shirt and clean pants.

The kettle's whistling some popular
song. I'll drink tea like an Englishman
and eat a Polish sweet roll. My mother
brought it yesterday, slightly burned.

The baker gaped at the legs of his
new one, just learning to spread,
royal icing and buttercream too,
so everyone is getting it for free.

Streets are annoyingly busy
and Christmas is coming soon.
You're everywhere I look.
I hope you're happy now.

Synecdoche

Sam Risebrow

If he had understood thermodynamics
he would have known exactly what was happening,
and how it was happening,
when she tipped the steaming contents of a kettle in his cup
and let the liquid soak into the teabag.
He just watched
while the water transformed itself tobacco-brown,
translucent, earthy, slightly spiced,
and sweated billowed vapor out, then off in wisps
that disappeared,
like the last atoms will collapse when the world has ended.
He would have understood why practice makes perfect—
and why people need time to adjust
to one another sometimes;
like in his first year at university
when he was lonely.

If he had understood drama
he would have known exactly why,
and how,
she had made him, in that moment, feel afraid
that he'd let down his grandma.
All he heard was rippling—
while neither said a word.
He would have understood how Alfred Hitchcock,
or Poe, or Goya make you want
to beg some type of god to make the world less empty.

He would have understood hard drugs,
why his grandmother was so opposed to them,
and why pictures of terrified brown people
had made her vote Brexit.
He would have understood why the government can open
his emails
and why mankind actually isn't capable of learning
from history.

If he had understood why she really disapproved,
he would have understood exactly why,
and how,
emotions cloud our mind sometimes;
viruses,
deleting information,
like book burners.
He would have understood exactly why
the House of Wisdom one day dyed the Tigris,
what it means to be in a community,
Leviticus,
and the Romanization of Spain.

If he had understood how tea became so popular in England—
for a Chinese plant farmed in India—
he would have known exactly why,
and how,
some people came to say that tea's an art
while some say science.
He would have understood roots;
those probing, fragile fingers, and how
the acrid, sour butter, salty smell outside McDonald's
makes you crave a beige and soggy meal.

He would have understood Hollywood,
fractal mathematics,
and why the dinosaurs starved.

If he had understood neurotransmitters,
he would have known exactly why,
and how,
a cup of tea could leave him so exhausted.
He also would have known exactly why
he thought that
being with Rumena would be worth that conversation—
why he thought about her quite so often, now,
and why his palms got sweaty
outside in the cold
on the days he waited for her at the station.
He would have understood
exactly how information is transferred, extrapolated
and forgotten.
How caffeine is diluted, drank, absorbed,
and then transported to the brain cells—
which need a little help, sometimes, to soak in
everything that's happening—
when our lives get quite confusing,
like the world.

Winter Warmth

Luciana Francis

Summer is an open letter we read
again and again.

With autumn comes the folding
of its scented paper;

we put it back in an envelope
clad in stars and snow.

One hand against the windowpane,
while another holds a slice of apple pie—

little crumbs gather among the glitter
from baubles set off by tea lights.

Toward December, the year curls up small,
cradled in myrrh and frankincense,

like a newborn, wide-eyed and in awe
of everything that's yet to come.

Winter Song

Luciana Francis

Until the very first crocus
breaks through the ground

we hold fort, we stay closer;
we hold hands and we sing songs.

It's been a long way to here, little one,
and the table is set to celebrate

every single blessing in our lives—
this is our home:

where we are together,
where we light the humble fire,

where we hang our coats and hats;
where we leave a glass of milk,

some carrots, and a plate of cookies
by the muddy boots on our welcome mat.

Lunch Date

Katrina Agbayani

They don't sleep in the same bed anymore, but they still eat lunch at Mitsume's on Thursday afternoons. They walk in silence to the restaurant and pick the same table toward the back, where the only out-of-commission light fixture hangs uselessly. They spend the first fifteen minutes coughing into their elbows and readjusting their collars. Ralph wears his lush cashmere sweater under his threadbare, fifteen-year-old winter coat. Sarah turns her wedding band over and over on her finger.

On the way in, they passed a young mother with her two children snuggled in a booth, their cherubic faces smeared with food. Sarah hears the gurgles and coos of the babies behind her and remembers when they had Johnny's first birthday here, the extra benches and chairs being brought out from the wood paneled storage wall beside them. Sarah leans in to tell Ralph about the memory of all those parties that never seem to happen anymore but hesitates as Ralph blinks the sun out of his cloudy eyes. Sarah remains hunched forward even as the memory of streamers and singing and candlelight turn as thin as the yellow paint that exposes the lumps in the wall.

She arranges her hands neatly on the table. The table's sticky with food splatter that couldn't be wiped off with the wet cloth: the drips of yesterday's Coca-Cola and the smear of chili oil. The seats are warm. Outside, the cold winter sun is harsh and white but turning golden at the edges.

"Lovely day," Ralph says, checking his watch. Its leather strap is brown as dry, loose dirt, worn from forty years of wear.

"Lovely day," Sarah says with a tight smile.

"I might be trying the beef today."

Sarah raises her eyebrows. "Oh?"

"Might try something new."

Sarah opens her mouth to tease him—some joke about his use of *might*, how it dooms him already—but the flash of his watch stops her. The hands stay still, useless.

Sarah got Ralph the watch as a wedding gift. She surprised him with it on the morning after their wedding day, in the cramped apartment they would rent for another year and a half before moving into their starter home. No time or money for a honeymoon—their breakfast that morning was leftover cake. The lukewarm milk was clumpy at the edges, and Ralph had let the coffee percolate too long; the harsh shine of the wedding made each of them sloppy when the festivities ended. Forty years later and Sarah's mouth fills with the oily sweetness of stale frosting and the bitter film of black coffee.

Their waitress's hair is coffee-dark and bouncy on her shoulders. She comes over to ask them if their usual has changed, and Sarah looks pointedly at Ralph, whose face crumples as he admits that it hasn't. *It'll be right out*, she assures, leaving them to their choreographed fidgeting. Sarah does not bring up the beef, or the watch. Ralph adjusts the cuffs of his shirt sleeves over and over. Watching him gives Sarah a sudden itch.

"Johnny and his girlfriend are visiting next week," Sarah says, breaching the silence like a hiker breaking the hush of the summit with a desperate breath. "They'll need the guest room."

Ralph huffs but does not protest. His cheeks redden, which he tries to hide by his dramatic pouring of the tea. Ralph did a lot of odd jobs around the neighborhood before working steady at the hydro company. It barely paid the bills, but Sarah loved it at first. Ralph would always come home smelling of grass, or sometimes rain. If Sarah smelled green in the air, that meant either Ralph or spring was nearby. In his current age, Ralph was susceptible to ailments that required a rotation of prescribed ointments. Sarah would cringe in bed next to Ralph and his sharp, sterile scents. It was the final straw leading to the separate beds. Still, old habits die hard. Every Thursday, the first cup of tea Ralph pours is always for Sarah.

"It's hot," Ralph warns.

"God forbid."

"What?" The line between Ralph's eyebrows deepens with his confusion. Over the years, the lines in his face toughened like scar tissue. "Did you want it cold?"

"I was joking."

"Oh."

Ralph considers it for a moment, then chuckles to himself. Sarah leans forward, pleased and pink as the peeling paint on the north side of the room.

Sarah sips the tea, remembering Ralph's chemical scent. How it frightened her when the smell was in her hair in the morning, although she spent the night untouched. She looks at her hands, which are suddenly so small around the tea mug. She wonders how she had gotten here, in this body. Across from her, Ralph folds, then unfolds his napkin.

In the air hangs the scent of the ramen they ordered, thickening just beyond the double doors of the kitchen. The crash of the pans and hiss of the stove are promises of the meal ahead. Eagerly, without meaning to, Sarah and Ralph perk their heads toward the scent and the sounds. Soy and salt and the richness of miso is almost on the tongue, but not quite. Just outside the window is spring, but not quite. The walls, empty of shadows, are tiled with the same shade of green as the walls of a high school cafeteria.

On Johnny's graduation day, Ralph and Sarah waited in his school cafeteria while he cleaned out the last relics from his locker. The walls were scaled in green tiles. Sarah walked around scouring for vandalism: various initials enclosed in Sharpie hearts, unrepeatable obscenities carved with the blade of a geometry compass. Ralph sat at a nearby table watching her as she walked, arms behind her back like an art gallery patron.

"I'd be sitting here," Ralph said after clearing his voice. "I'd be sitting here at lunch and you'd sit a ways away with your girlfriends, just like that."

Sarah took a seat at the nearest table, playing along. "Just like this," she said, smiling. Laughter floated in from the front door. The fluorescent lights buzzed above them like mechanical cicadas in a mechanical summer.

"Our son is going to college," Ralph said quietly, looking away. "We were just here, Sarah. Just here."

The bouncy-haired waitress returns with bowls big enough to swim in, and Sarah breaks out of her reverie with the clang of ceramic on wood. Across from her, the steam clouds Ralph's face, obstructing it. Sarah momentarily forgets what Ralph looks like, but this does not frighten her. No ailment of the mind or body could obstruct Sarah's recognition of Ralph. She would know him by the shift of the air, by the texture of the quiet he brings. The steam lifts, and Sarah quietly rejoices.

"Here," Sarah says, taking the soft-boiled egg in her soup and depositing it carefully into Ralph's bowl.

"Thank you," Ralph says, nodding slightly. Between his chopsticks is his serving of bean sprouts, which he gives to Sarah wordlessly.

"Lovely meal," she observes.

"Very lovely. Very lovely."

Somehow, the meal is devoured. Somehow, the couple will walk out into the afternoon, just like every Thursday beforehand, which is so ordinary but so necessary. As is the hand that finds another and holds it.

A Warm Bond

Vaishnavi Anand

I met you when we were both old enough
to know how different we were.
We were standing on a footpath
I remember seeing your breath dance white
and brown eyes glance at the pale sun peeking
through the clouds when you spoke next.
You only remember smiling at my hand tucked into your jacket.
I wished for hot chocolate,
you asked if I liked ice cream.
You didn't notice my sigh in the white laugh.
I wish I knew how anybody ate ice cream in the cold—
perhaps you were winter's son returning with a cone.
The wind picked up and you slipped,
pulling me to the cold ground with you,
but I could still feel the warmth from that ice cream,
the small piece of warmth you were giving me.

We laughed after we fell
and made angels lying on a
stony path with meager snow.
You said the snow told you
that we should have hot chocolate
from that rundown old man in a roadside shop
who looked like he made milk from the snow.
I said okay
only to hold that
hot chocolate's warmth in my memory
beyond that one winter's cold.

You told me later
a tradition begins by grabbing on to a small
feeling we want to safeguard
for a lifetime and beyond.
I always believed you wholeheartedly.

Five winters ahead,
we laugh together, holding cups of hot chocolate,
about how we believed a warm bond
could be bought,
or that a bond is born in spite of unspoken thoughts,
that warmth could be found anywhere but our own hearts.

a tradition begins by grabbing on to a small feeling we want to safeguard for a lifetime and beyond

Contributors

Katrina Agbayani is an editor with *Acta Victoriana* and *La Mosaic*. Her poems have been published in *SAND Journal*, *UC Review*, and *The Trinity Review* and have been awarded the OECTA Young Authors Award.

Vaishnavi Anand (she/her) is an Indian student and poet (and cat mom) pursuing her undergraduate studies in information technology. In her free time, she's absorbed in writing poetry or bird photography. You can find her work forthcoming in *Sledgehammer Lit* and on Instagram at @thevariegatedpen.

Fran Fernández Arce (she/her) is a Chilean poet living in Suffolk, England. Her work has been published or is forthcoming in *Pollux Journal*, *Catatonic Daughters*, and *Firmament*, among others. She is a poetry reader for *The Walled City Journal* and poetry editor for *Moonflake Press*. She enjoys reading and writing about art, language, and the weather outside her window.

A. M. Arndt has been a child, a sibling, a parent, a spouse, a lover, a teacher, an artist, and a dreamer. Through it all, A. M. Arndt has been a writer, focusing mostly on prose poetry. This poet has been recognized by the Dorothy Sargent Rosenberg Poetry Contest and has had the poem "Hemingway" published in *Into the Void*.

Tomas Baiza is originally from San José, California, and now lives in Boise, Idaho. He is a Pushcart-nominated writer whose work has appeared or is forthcoming in *Parhelion*, *Meniscus*, *PANK Magazine*, *101 Proof Horror*, *The Meadow*, *Peatsmoke*, *The Good Life Review*, *Kelp Journal*, Black Lawrence Press, *Bacopa Literary Review*, *Passengers Journal*, and elsewhere. Tomas's first novel, *Deliver Me: A Pocho's Accidental Guide to*

College, Love, and Pizza Delivery, and his short fiction collection, *A Purpose to Our Savagery: Stories and Poems*, will appear from Running Wild/RIZE Press in 2022.

Wendy BooydeGraaff has fiction, poems, and essays included in *Not Very Quiet*, *Another Chicago Magazine*, *The Journal of Compressed Creative Arts*, *NOON*, and elsewhere. Born and raised in Ontario, Canada, she now lives in Michigan.

Ellen Clayton is from Suffolk, England, where she lives with her husband and three young children. Her poetry often focuses on motherhood and love. She has recently been published in *The Daily Drunk*, *Discretionary Love*, and *Gypsophila* and has poems forthcoming in *Tattie Zine*, *Nightingale and Sparrow*, *Corporeal*, and *Honeyfire Literary Magazine*. Her poetry can be found on Instagram at @ellen_writes_poems.

Sara Davis is a recovering academic and marketing writer who lives in Philadelphia with two elderly cats. Her PhD in American literature is from Temple University. She has recently published flash in *Cleaver Magazine*, *Toho Journal*, and *CRAFT* literary magazine. She blogs about books and climate anxiety at literarysara.net. You can find her at @LiterarySara.

Steve Denehan lives in Kildare, Ireland, with his wife Eimear and daughter Robin. He is the author of two chapbooks and two poetry collections. Twice winner of *Irish Times'* New Irish Writing, he has numerous publication credits, including *Poetry Ireland Review*, *Acumen*, *Prairie Fire*, *Westerly*, and *Into the Void*.

Laine Derr holds an MFA from Northern Arizona University and has published interviews with Carl Phillips, Ross Gay, and Ted Kooser. Recent work appears or is forthcoming in *Antithesis*, *Portland Review*, *North Dakota Quarterly*, *Prairie Schooner*, and elsewhere.

Jaime Dill (she/her) is an accomplished book coach, founder of Polish & Pitch editorial agency, and editor-in-chief of Cardigan Press who uses her precious downtime to pour her lesser-known self into free verse poetry. Jaime's writing reflects her professional interest in language while also ripping apart the rules to show the world the raw beauty of emotion, femininity, and admission.

Tamiko Dooley is a half-Japanese mother of two. She read Latin and French at New College, Oxford. When there's no pandemic, she's hired as a wedding pianist from time to time.

Nicole Farmer is a writer and teacher living in Asheville, North Carolina. Her poems have been published in *Sheepshead Review*, *The Bangalore Review*, *The Roadrunner Review*, *Wild Roof Journal*, *Bacopa Literary Review*, *The Great Smokies Review*, *KAKALAK*, *86 Logic*, *Wingless Dreamer*, and others. Her play *50 JOBS* was produced in Los Angeles. Nicole was awarded the 2021 First Prize in Prose Poetry from *Bacopa Literary Review*. Way back in the nineties, she graduated from The Juilliard School of Drama. You can find her dancing barefoot in her driveway on the full moon at midnight.

Jen Feroze (she/her) lives by the sea in Essex, United Kingdom, with her husband and two small sleep thieves. Her work has recently appeared in *Doghouse Press*, *Gingernut* magazine, and The Mum Poem Press. Her debut collection, *The Colour of Hope*, was published in 2020. She loves turquoise things, Christmas lights, and cheese you can eat with a spoon. Find her on Instagram at @the_colourofhope and on Twitter at @jenlareine.

Agnieszka Filipek is a Polish-born poet living in Ireland. Her work has appeared in over sixty publications internationally, including countries such as Poland, Ireland, India, China, Bangladesh, England, Wales, Northern Ireland, Germany, Canada, and the United States. Her poems have appeared in *The Journal of Compressed Creative Arts*, *Lucent Dreaming*, *Black Bough Poetry*, *Crannóg*, *The Blue Nib*, *Chrysanthemum*, *Marble Poetry*, *Headway Quarterly*, and elsewhere. She has a poetry Facebook page dedicated to her writing at facebook.com/polmnieapoltobie.

Joshua Flores manifested in Chicago with Spanish as his first language, and the struggle to learn English well led him to read. At ten years old, he pecked out short stories on an old electric typewriter. He hasn't stopped writing since.

Luciana Francis (she/her) is a Brazilian-born, UK-based writer of poetry and fiction. She earned a BA (hons) degree in anthropology and media from Goldsmiths, University of London. Her writing has appeared in *Popshot Quarterly*, *Kissing Dynamite*, *Whale Road Review*, and *Literary Mama*, among others, and is forthcoming in *Choices*, the fourth issue of Mum Poet Club zine, edited by British poet Liz Berry, and in *Cōnfingō Magazine*.

Alex Grehy has a sweet life filled with narrowboating, rescue greyhounds, singing, and chocolate. Her work has been published worldwide, including a recipe and memoir in the Red Penguin Books cookery anthology *Feeding the Flock*. Her vivid prose, thought-provoking poetry, and original view of the world has led to her best friend to say, "For someone so lovely, you're very twisted!"

Larry Griggs got an English degree from the University of West Georgia before he decided to start writing. Then in a spur-of-the-moment decision, he went back to work on his MAT. He has a passion for food and eating, and in his downtime he likes to cook and find good restaurants to eat at.

Sheryl Guterl writes from New Mexico and New Hampshire. Retiring to the Southwest after a career as an educator in New Jersey, she appreciates more sunshine, higher mountains, and less winter ice. Her cabin on a lake in wooded New England provides inspiration and refreshment with cooler summers. Sheryl's poetry is found in *The RavensPerch*, *Iris Literary Journal*, *Deep Wild Journal*, *Bethlehem Writers Roundtable*, *Poetic Sun*, *Mason Street Review*, and several local anthologies.

Charlotte Gutzmer is a nonbinary twenty-one-year-old undergraduate writer fascinated with all things magical and bizarre. In their craft, they explore themes of fantasy, identity, environment, and myths—they especially adore creating uncanny worlds that explore surrealism, obscurity, and realms just beyond our reach. Charlotte's goal is to draw readers into surreal worlds and to help them realize that it's okay to face the darkness. It's often there that we find the most obscure and precious magic.

Ceinwen E Cariad Haydon lives in Newcastle upon Tyne, United Kingdom, and writes short stories and poetry. She has been widely published in web magazines and in print anthologies and is a Pushcart Prize and Forward Prize nominee. She is developing a practice as a participatory arts facilitator and believes everyone's voice counts.

C. T. Holte grew up in Minnesota without color TV; played along creeks and in cornfields; went to lots of school; and has had gigs as teacher, editor, and less wordy things. He recently migrated to New Mexico and got a cool electric chainsaw for Christmas. His poetry has been published in *Words*, *California Quarterly*, *Months to Years*, *Pensive: A Global Journal of Spirituality and the Arts*, *Mediterranean Poetry*, *The Daily Drunk*, and elsewhere and has been hung from trees to celebrate the Rio Grande Bosque.

Amanda Hurley is a writer, translator, and editor, originally from Wellington, New Zealand. These days, she lives in a small town surrounded by lakes and forest in former East Germany, where she co-runs a cafe with her partner. She has previously worked for Radio New Zealand and the *Daily Telegraph* in London.

Rachel Kim hails from somewhere between Seoul, South Korea, and New Jersey. She is a senior at the University of California, Berkeley, with undergraduate majors in media studies and psychology. She seeks to find the special in the mundane through writing, film, and photography.

Aral L. is a nonbinary latinx poet living in Canada. They are a student and dream of nothing more than writing.

Annie Marhefka is a writer, HR consultant, and mama residing in Baltimore, Maryland, with her husband and daughter. She thrives on coffee, relationships, and delving into deep, dark, swirly feelings. She also serves as executive director of Yellow Arrow Publishing Co., which supports women-identifying writers in Baltimore.

Ciera Horton McElroy has work in *AGNI*, *Bridge Eight*, *Crab Orchard Review*, *Little Fiction*, *Lumina*, and *Flash Fiction Magazine*, among others. She is represented by Folio Literary Management.

Maggi McGettigan (she/her) is writing from Chester County, Pennsylvania. Her work can be found most recently in the literary magazine *CONCINNITY* from Downingtown Books and on maggimcgettigan.com.

Kay Miller resides in Cleveland, Ohio, with her husband and two adult children. She enjoys writing short stories and poetry and is working on a full-length cozy mystery.

Mark J. Mitchell was born in Chicago and grew up in Southern California. His latest poetry collection, *Roshi San Francisco*, was just published by Norfolk Publishing. *Starting from Tu Fu* was recently published by Encircle Publications. He lives in San Francisco with his wife, the activist and documentarian Joan Juster, where he made his marginal living pointing out pretty things. Now, like everyone else, he's unemployed. He has published two novels, three chapbooks, and two full-length collections so far. His first chapbook won the Negative Capability Award. A meager online presence can be found on Facebook at @MarkJMitchellwriter, and he sometimes tweets at @MarkJMitchellSF. A primitive website now exists at mark-j-mitchell.square.site.

Sam Risebrow was born in London and lived in Scotland most of his adult life, where he studied English at Stirling University. He now lives in Madrid, where he teaches English as a second language to children and adults. He has been writing poetry for around fifteen years but has only recently decided to submit a small number of poems for publication. He was longlisted for the Plough Prize in spring 2021.

Philip Styrt (he/him) lives in Davenport, Iowa, with his wife, toddler, and toothless dog. His poetry unites recognizable and traditional forms of meter and rhyme within a distinctively modern sensibility. His work has been published in, among others, *carte blanche*, *Eastern Iowa Review*, and *Writers Resist*, and he recently won a regional prize in the 2021 Maria W. Faust Sonnet Contest.

Lizzie Thornton graduated from the University of South Carolina with a BA in English. Since then, she has turned her focus to her own editing and publishing career, establishing her freelance editing company, Lady Lizzie Editing, and co-founding Cardigan Press, an up-and-coming small press. She has continued writing for herself (mainly poetry and a novel that will eventually get finished), but this is the first time she has been published officially. She hopes this is the first of many publications to come. You can find her on Twitter and Instagram at @iamladylizzie.

Kalisse L. Van Dellen writes about where she's been and what she's lost. She is a graduate of Belhaven University in

Jackson, Mississippi, and resides as a Canadian expatriate in Greenville, South Carolina. Her work has most recently been featured in *3 Moon Magazine*, *the Brogue*, and *Mississippi's Best Emerging Poets.*

Sean Wang (he/him) is in Singapore on national service. His poetry has been published, and he works as a writer and editor on the side. He can be found on Instagram at @wean_sang.

Alexandra Weiss writes in Chicago, where their apartment is slowly being taken over by Halloween decorations and houseplants. They edit for *Another Chicago Magazine* and have work published or forthcoming in *From the Depths*, *Coffin Bell*, *Giving Room Mag*, and others.

Skye Wilson is a Scottish writer with an MSc in creative writing from the University of Edinburgh. She has been described as "an ugly feminist bitch" and thinks two out of three is not bad. Skye loves rugby, words, and ugly shirts. Find more of her work at skye-wilson.com.

Luna Yin is a fourteen-year-old poet who was born in China and lives in Canada. Luna credits her wild imagination and love of writing to a life spent moving between countries and reading fantasy novels. When she isn't spending rainy days lounging on the sofa with a good thriller, Luna is often sitting by her piano and trying to turn her thoughts into sheet music. You can find her on Instagram at @luna.y.writes.

Editorial Staff

Natasha Lioe, Founder and Publisher

Natasha Lioe graduated with a BA in narrative studies from University of Southern California. She's always had an affinity for words and stories and emotions. Her work has appeared in *Adsum Literary Magazine*, and she won the Edward B. Moses Creative Writing Competition in 2016. Her greatest strength is finding and focusing the pathos in an otherwise cold world, and she hopes to help humans tell their unique, compelling stories.

Carolina VonKampen, Publisher and Editor in Chief

Carolina VonKampen graduated with a BA in English and history and completed the University of Chicago's editing certificate program. She is available for hire as a freelance editor. For more information on her freelance work, visit carolina vonkampen.com. Her writing has appeared in *So to Speak*'s blog, *FIVE:2:ONE*'s #thesideshow, *Moonchild Magazine*, and *Déraciné Magazine*. Her short story "Logan Paul Is Dead" was nominated by *Dream Pop Journal* for the 2018 Best of the Net. She tweets about editing at @carolinamarie_v and talks about books she's reading on Instagram at @carolinamariereads.

April Bayer, Reader

April Bayer is an MA student in English literature at the University of South Dakota. She graduated with high distinction from Concordia University, Nebraska in 2019 with a BA in English and theology and a BS Ed in educational studies. When she isn't busy teaching her students about literature and composition, she enjoys writing poetry, playing with cats, and researching the works of Willa Cather. Her work has previously appeared in *Potpourri* and *Capsule Stories Isolation Edition*. April joined *Capsule Stories* as a reader in November 2020.

Stephanie Coley, Reader

Stephanie Coley is a country girl from Gering, Nebraska. She graduated in 2016 from Concordia University, Nebraska with a BA in English and a minor in art. She has been a journalism teacher, janitor, data technician, and more. Stephanie is a published poet, appearing in the National Creativity Series of 2009 and *Mango* Issue 3, Respeto, in 2017. She is also a winner of the 2020 Historic Posters Reimagined Project, which can be found at the Nebraska History Museum in Lincoln, Nebraska. Stephanie currently works as the program manager at the West Nebraska Arts Center in Scottsbluff, Nebraska. Stephanie joined *Capsule Stories* as a reader in January 2021.

Rhea Dhanbhoora, Reader

Rhea Dhanbhoora worked for close to a decade as an editor and writer before quitting her job and moving to New York to get her master's degree and finally writing the stories everyone told her no one would ever read. Her debut poetry collection, *Sandalwood-Scented Skeletons*, is forthcoming from Finishing Line Press in 2022. Her work has appeared or is forthcoming in publications such as *Sparkle & Blink*, *Awakened Voices*, *Five on the Fifth*, *Capsule Stories Autumn 2020 Edition*, *Fly on the Wall Press*, *HerStry*, *Artsy*, *Broccoli Mag*, and *JMWW*. Her work has been nominated for a Pushcart Prize and Best American Essays. She is currently on the board of directors for the literary organization Quiet Lightning and editor of RealBrownTalk. Rhea joined *Capsule Stories* as a reader in January 2021. She's working on several projects, including a linked story collection about women based in the underrepresented Parsi Zoroastrian diaspora. You can read her work online at rheadhanbhoora.com.

Hannah Fortna, Reader

Hannah Fortna graduated in 2016 from Concordia University, Nebraska, combining her passion for the written word and her affinity for art making with a degree in English and a minor in photography. After a three-year career as a freelance copyeditor, she heard traveling calling her name and now works seasonal jobs in places connected to America's national parks. When she's not selling souvenirs to tourists in gift shops, she enjoys hiking, photographing natural spaces, and writing about the flora and fauna she saw while on the trail. She reads anything from poetry to middle-grade novels, but the nature-inspired creative nonfiction section is her haunt in any bookstore. Her poetry has previously appeared in *Moonchild Magazine* and *Capsule Stories Spring 2019 Edition*. Hannah joined *Capsule Stories* as a reader in November 2020.

Kendra Nuttall, Reader

Kendra Nuttall is a copywriter by day and poet by night. She has a BA in English with an emphasis in creative writing from Utah Valley University. Her work has previously appeared in *Spectrum*, *Capsule Stories*, *Chiron Review*, and *What Rough Beast*, as well as various other journals and anthologies. She is the author of the poetry collections *A Statistical Study of Randomness* (Finishing Line Press, 2021) and *Our Bones Ache Together* (FlowerSong Press, forthcoming). Kendra lives in Utah with her husband and poodle. When she's not writing, you can find her hiking, watching reality TV, or attempting to pet every animal she sees. You can find out more about her work at kendranuttall.com. Kendra joined *Capsule Stories* as a reader in January 2021.

Rachel Skelton, Reader

Rachel Skelton graduated from William Woods University with a BA in English, a concentration in writing, and a secondary major in business administration, a concentration in management. She has interned for Dzanc Books and now works as a freelance fiction editor specializing in speculative fiction. You can find more information about her work at theeditingskeleton.com. She occasionally tweets about editing at @EditingSkeleton and talks about books she's reading at @TheReadingSkeleton on Instagram. When she's not doing anything reading-related, she's hanging out with her cats, collecting houseplants, and attempting to learn how to crochet. Rachel joined *Capsule Stories* as a reader in January 2021.

Deanne Sleet, Reader

Deanne Sleet is a graduate of Saint Louis University with a BA in English, a concentration in creative writing, and minors in African American studies and women's and gender studies. She has interned for *River Styx* and Midwest Artist Project Services, where she gained experience with grant writing, editing, and writing copy. She is currently the leasing and marketing manager at City Lofts on Laclede and holds the secretary position for SLU's Black Alumni Association. She writes short fiction and poetry, and a novel is in the making. In her spare time, she hangs out with her cat and roller-skates. Deanne joined *Capsule Stories* as a reader in February 2021.

Claire Taylor, Reader

Claire Taylor is a writer in Baltimore, Maryland, where she lives with her husband, son, a bossy old cat, and an anxious dog who longs to be the cat's best friend. Claire's writing has appeared in a variety of publications, and she was a finalist for the 2020 Lascaux Prize in Poetry and winner of the 2021 *Serotonin* New Year's Day poetry competition. Her micro-chapbook, *A History of Rats*, is available from Ghost City Press. Claire is the founder and editor in chief of *Little Thoughts Press*, a print literary magazine of writing for and by kids. Claire joined *Capsule Stories* as a reader in March 2021. A selection of Claire's work is available online at clairemtaylor.com.

Submission Guidelines

Capsule Stories is a print literary magazine published once every season. Our first issue was published on March 1, 2019, and we accept submissions year-round.

Become published in a literary magazine run by like-minded people. We have a penchant for pretty words, an affinity to the melancholy, and an undeniably time-ful aura. We believe that stories exist in a specific moment, and that that moment is what makes those stories unique.

What we're really looking for are stories that can touch the heart. Stories that come from the heart. Stories about love, identity, the self, the world, the human condition. Stories that show what living in this world as the human you are is like.

We accept short stories, poems, and remarkably written essays. For short stories and essays, we're interested in pieces under 3,000 words. You may include up to five poems in a single poetry submission (please send them all in one Word document), and only send one story or essay at a time. Please send previously unpublished work only—a piece is considered published if it has been posted or made publicly available on a blog, website, or social media platform. You may only submit one submission per edition. Simultaneous submissions are okay, but please let us know if your submission is accepted elsewhere. Please include a brief third-person bio with your submission, and attach your submissions in a Word document (no PDFs unless your poetry has very specific formatting, please!).

Find our full submission guidelines and current theme descriptions at capsulestories.com/submissions.

Connect with us!
capsulestories.com
@CapsuleStories on Twitter and Facebook
@CapsuleStoriesMag on Instagram

www.ingramcontent.com/pod-product-compliance
Lightning Source LLC
Chambersburg PA
CBHW040529170726
48295CB00012B/401
* 9 7 8 1 9 5 3 9 5 8 1 0 5 *